# The Rich Boy

F. Scott Fitzgerald

ET REMOTISSIMA PROPE

**100 PAGES**

100 PAGES

Published by Hesperus Press Limited

4 Rickett Street, London SW6 1RU

www.hesperuspress.com

'The Rich Boy' first published in 1926 in *Redbook Magazine*;
'The Bridal Party' first published in 1929 in *The Saturday Evening Post*;
'The Last of the Belles' first published in 1929 in *The Saturday Evening Post*;
This collection first published by Hesperus Press Limited, 2003

Designed and typeset by Fraser Muggeridge
Printed in the United Arab Emirates by Oriental Press

ISBN: 1-84391-045-4

# CONTENTS

# FOREWORD

'The Rich Boy', one of Fitzgerald's more ambitious and deeply felt short stories, contains a sentence that occasioned a tiff between the author and his formidable friend and rival, Ernest Hemingway. In August of 1936, after Fitzgerald had confessed in print the low ebb of his fortunes and mental condition, *Esquire* published a Hemingway story, 'The Snows of Kilimanjaro', containing this passage from the autobiographical hero's thought-stream:

> 'The rich were dull and they drank too much or they played too much backgammon. They were dull and they were repetitious. He remembered poor Scott Fitzgerald and his romantic awe of them and how he had started a story once that began, "The rich are different from you and me." And how someone had said to Scott, Yes, they have more money. But that was not humorous to Scott. He thought they were a special glamorous race and when he found they weren't it wrecked him just as much as any other thing that wrecked him.'

Fitzgerald, living at the time in Ashville, North Carolina, was quick to respond, in a letter as gracious as it was blunt:

> *Dear Ernest,*
> *Please lay off me in print. If I choose to write* de profundis *sometimes it doesn't mean I want friends praying aloud over my corpse. No doubt you meant it kindly but it cost me a night's sleep. And when you incorporate it (the story) in a book would you mind cutting my name?*

When the story appeared in a Hemingway collection, the name had been changed to Julian. This was at the insistence of Maxwell Perkins, the editor at Scribner's of both men, according to the scholar Matthew Bruccoli, in a long footnote in his *F. Scott Fitzgerald: A Life in Letters*. Bruccoli claims that the object of the put-down had been not Fitzgerald but Hemingway himself, bragging 'I am getting to know the rich' at a luncheon with Perkins and the critic Mary Colum, who had then said, 'The only difference between the rich and other people is that the rich have more money.'

In any case, it is not much of a put-down, and Hemingway's self-serving account ignores the next sentence in 'The Rich Boy', which begins to explain the difference:

'They possess and enjoy early, and it does something to them, makes them soft where we are hard, and cynical where we are trustful, in a way that, unless you were born rich, it is very difficult to understand.'

It was important to Fitzgerald to try to understand. Literary pilgrims to St Paul can still see the modest houses his struggling, shabby-genteel parents rented in the vicinity of (but rarely on) Summit Avenue, the street of the local rich. His father, a delicate man whom he physically resembled, was descended from Maryland aristocracy, including Francis Scott Key, the writer of 'The Star-Spangled Banner', but Edward Fitzgerald lacked the drive and vitality to be a successful businessman. Scott's mother, born Molly McQuillan, brought a fierce Irish Catholicism and some money – inherited from her immigrant father, a grocer – to the marriage, but only enough to cling to the edges of respectability, and to send her son to private school and

Princeton. At Princeton, Fitzgerald associated with the sons of the rich, and his short stories for *The Saturday Evening Post* made him, for a time, wealthy, but he and his reckless wife, Zelda, had no gift for accumulating money; in 1924 he wrote for the *Post* a comic essay, 'How to Live on $36,000 a Year', when this was a fortune. Financial security eluded him just as his glamorous heroines elude his heroes. Jay Gatsby does not know, but the reader can see, that Daisy will always choose, over her old suitor's quixotic devotion and flashy, shady semblance of wealth, the secure protection of her brutish husband, who is truly rich.

The other famous aphorism on the first page of 'The Rich Boy' is:

'Begin with an individual, and before you know it you find that you have created a type; begin with a type, and you find that you have created – nothing.'

Yet, though Fitzgerald closely based Anson Hunter on his hard-drinking Princeton friend Ludlow Fowler – 'It is in a large measure the story of your life,' he ingenuously wrote to Fowler in 1925, 'toned down here and there and simplified' – the rich boy retains something of the rotundity and vagueness of a type. Increasingly plump because of his drinking, he becomes, out of the wreck of his two main romances, a womaniser compulsively seeking the flattery his sense of inherent superiority demands. That sense, presumably, made him incapable of popping the question to Paula Legendre, preferring to keep her as a legend of lost love, or of consummating his romance with the sporty, less idealised Dolly Karger. Anson has, in his privileged vanity, a sterilising touch, killing the harmless affair between his Aunt Edna and a young man much like himself but without the clout of his money.

Fitzgerald was a considerable student of how money functioned. Anson, at first a dynamic and bluff and shrewd performer in the brokerage house he joins, acquires, touchingly, the 'fussy pessimism of a man of forty', and is urged by his firm to take a vacation, since 'on every transaction in which he was involved he acted as a drag and a strain'. 'The Bridal Party' portrays, in the person of Hamilton Rutherford, a more buoyant and successful type, who no sooner goes broke in a stock-market downturn than he is offered a fifty-thousand-dollar-a-year job: 'He happens to have it – that young man… In another year he'll be back with the millionaires.' Also, he carries off the girl. To Fitzgerald, money signals animal vitality; sexual success is part of its romance. But, by his own inner lights, sexual success wasn't worth celebrating; it had something coarse about it.

His typical heroes mourn the loss of their true loves, usually met in the heady Southern atmosphere of magnolias and moonlight evoked in 'The Last of the Belles'. In his own life he *did* get the girl – spectacular, beautiful Zelda from Montgomery, Alabama – and for a spell they were the ultimate Jazz-Age couple. But she became a mentally troubled liability, and the difficulties and disappointments of possessing the love object defied even Fitzgerald's staunch and graceful descriptive powers. *Tender is the Night* tries to encompass his predicament, and cannot, for all its labour of polish, be called a successful novel; it does not master its own matter, as *The Great Gatsby*, through the agency of its bystander narrator, so satisfactorily does. 'The Rich Boy' was one of the few works to come out of the hectic year and a half, from April 1925 to December 1926, that Scott and

Zelda spent in Paris after *Gatsby*'s completion. We can feel in it, for all its earnest, ruminative care, how difficult it was becoming for Fitzgerald, once so fabulously fluent, to write – to bring his susceptibility to romantic inertia and illusion into harmony with his clear-eyed, large-minded realism.

*– John Updike, 2003*

# The Rich Boy

Begin with an individual, and before you know it you find
that you have created a type; begin with a type, and you
find that you have created – nothing. That is because we are all
queer fish, queerer behind our faces and voices than we want
anyone to know or than we know ourselves. When I hear a
man proclaiming himself an 'average, honest, open fellow',
I feel pretty sure that he has some definite and perhaps
terrible abnormality which he has agreed to conceal – and his
protestation of being average and honest and open is his way
of reminding himself of his misprision.

There are no types, no plurals. There is a rich boy, and this
is his and not his brothers' story. All my life I have lived among
his brothers but this one has been my friend. Besides, if I
wrote about his brothers I should have to begin by attacking
all the lies that the poor have told about the rich and the rich
have told about themselves – such a wild structure they have
erected that when we pick up a book about the rich, some
instinct prepares us for unreality. Even the intelligent and
impassioned reporters of life have made the country of the rich
as unreal as fairy-land.

Let me tell you about the very rich. They are different from
you and me. They possess and enjoy early, and it does
something to them, makes them soft where we are hard, and
cynical where we are trustful, in a way that, unless you were
born rich, it is very difficult to understand. They think, deep
in their hearts, that they are better than we are because we had
to discover the compensations and refuges of life for ourselves.
Even when they enter deep into our world or sink below us,
they still think that they are better than we are. They are
different. The only way I can describe young Anson Hunter is

to approach him as if he were a foreigner and cling stubbornly to my point of view. If I accept his for a moment I am lost – I have nothing to show but a preposterous movie.

## 2

Anson was the eldest of six children who would some day divide a fortune of fifteen million dollars, and he reached the age of reason – is it seven? – at the beginning of the century when daring young women were already gliding along Fifth Avenue in electric 'mobiles'. In those days he and his brother had an English governess who spoke the language very clearly and crisply and well, so that the two boys grew to speak as she did – their words and sentences were all crisp and clear and not run together as ours are. They didn't talk exactly like English children but acquired an accent that is peculiar to fashionable people in the city of New York.

In the summer the six children were moved from the house on 71st Street to a big estate in northern Connecticut. It was not a fashionable locality – Anson's father wanted to delay as long as possible his children's knowledge of that side of life. He was a man somewhat superior to his class, which composed New York society, and to his period, which was the snobbish and formalised vulgarity of the Gilded Age, and he wanted his sons to learn habits of concentration and have sound constitutions and grow up into right-living and successful men. He and his wife kept an eye on them as well as they were able until the two older boys went away to school, but in huge establishments this is difficult – it was much simpler in the series of small and medium-sized houses in which my own youth was spent – I was never far out of the reach of my mother's voice, of the sense of her presence, her approval or disapproval.

Anson's first sense of his superiority came to him when he realised the half-grudging American deference that was paid to him in the Connecticut village. The parents of the boys he played with always enquired after his father and mother, and were vaguely excited when their own children were asked to the Hunters' house. He accepted this as the natural state of things, and a sort of impatience with all groups of which he was not the centre – in money, in position, in authority – remained with him for the rest of his life. He disdained to struggle with other boys for precedence – he expected it to be given him freely, and when it wasn't he withdrew into his family. His family was sufficient, for in the East money is still a somewhat feudal thing, a clan-forming thing. In the snobbish West, money separates families to form 'sets'.

At eighteen, when he went to New Haven, Anson was tall and thick-set, with a clear complexion and a healthy colour from the ordered life he had led in school. His hair was yellow and grew in a funny way on his head, his nose was beaked – these two things kept him from being handsome – but he had a confident charm and a certain brusque style, and the upper-class men who passed him on the street knew without being told that he was a rich boy and had gone to one of the best schools. Nevertheless, his very superiority kept him from being a success in college – the independence was mistaken for egotism, and the refusal to accept Yale standards with the proper awe seemed to belittle all those who had. So, long before he graduated, he began to shift the centre of his life to New York.

He was at home in New York – there was his own house with 'the kind of servants you can't get any more' – and his own family, of which, because of his good humour and a certain ability to make things go, he was rapidly becoming the centre, and the debutante parties, and the correct manly world of the men's clubs, and the occasional wild spree with the gallant girls whom New Haven only knew from the fifth row. His aspirations were conventional enough – they included even the irreproachable shadow he would some day marry, but they differed from the aspirations of the majority of young men in that there was no mist over them, none of that quality which is variously known as 'idealism' or 'illusion'. Anson accepted without reservation the world of high finance and high extravagance, of divorce and dissipation, of snobbery and of privilege. Most of our lives end as a compromise – it was as a compromise that his life began.

He and I first met in the late summer of 1917 when he was just out of Yale, and, like the rest of us, was swept up into the systematised hysteria of the war. In the blue-green uniform of the naval aviation he came down to Pensacola, where the hotel orchestras played 'I'm Sorry, Dear', and we young officers danced with the girls. Everyone liked him, and though he ran with the drinkers and wasn't an especially good pilot, even the instructors treated him with a certain respect. He was always having long talks with them in his confident, logical voice – talks which ended by his getting himself, or, more frequently, another officer, out of some impending trouble. He was convivial, bawdy, robustly avid for pleasure, and we were all surprised when he fell in love with a conservative and rather proper girl.

Her name was Paula Legendre, a dark, serious beauty from somewhere in California. Her family kept a winter residence just outside of town, and in spite of her primness she was enormously popular; there is a large class of men whose egotism can't endure humour in a woman. But Anson wasn't that sort, and I couldn't understand the attraction of her 'sincerity' – that was the thing to say about her – for his keen and somewhat sardonic mind.

Nevertheless, they fell in love – and on her terms. He no longer joined the twilight gathering at the De Soto Bar, and whenever they were seen together they were engaged in a long, serious dialogue, which must have gone on several weeks. Long afterwards he told me that it was not about anything in particular but was composed on both sides of immature and even meaningless statements – the emotional content that gradually came to fill it grew up not out of the words but out of its enormous seriousness. It was a sort of hypnosis. Often it was interrupted, giving way to that emasculated humour we call fun; when they were alone it was resumed again, solemn, low-keyed, and pitched so as to give each other a sense of unity in feeling and thought. They came to resent any interruptions of it, to be unresponsive to facetiousness about life, even to the mild cynicism of their contemporaries. They were only happy when the dialogue was going on, and its seriousness bathed them like the amber glow of an open fire. Towards the end there came an interruption they did not resent – it began to be interrupted by passion.

Oddly enough, Anson was as engrossed in the dialogue as she and as profoundly affected by it, yet at the same time aware that on his side much was insincere, and on hers much was merely simple. At first, too, he despised her emotional simplicity as well, but with his love her nature deepened and blossomed, and he could despise it no longer. He felt that if he could enter into Paula's warm safe life he would be happy. The long preparation of the dialogue removed any constraint – he taught her some of what he had learnt from more adventurous women, and she responded with a rapt holy intensity. One evening after a dance they agreed to marry, and he wrote a long letter about her to his mother. The next day Paula told him that she was rich, that she had a personal fortune of nearly a million dollars.

*3*

It was exactly as if they could say 'Neither of us has anything: we shall be poor together' – just as delightful that they should be rich instead. It gave them the same communion of adventure. Yet when Anson got leave in April, and Paula and her mother accompanied him North, she was impressed with the scale on which they lived. Alone with Anson for the first time in the room where he had played as a boy, she was filled with comfortable emotion, as though she were pre-eminently safe and taken care of. The pictures of Anson in a skullcap at his first school, of Anson on horseback with the sweetheart of a mysterious forgotten summer, of Anson in a gay group of ushers and bridesmaids at a wedding, made her jealous of his life apart from her in the past, and so completely did his authoritative person seem to sum up and typify these possessions of his that she was inspired with the idea of being married immediately and returning to Pensacola as his wife.

But an immediate marriage wasn't discussed – even the engagement was to be secret until after the war. When she realised that only two days of his leave remained, her dissatisfaction crystallised in the intention of making him as unwilling to wait as she was. They were driving to the country for dinner and she determined to force the issue that night.

Now a cousin of Paula's was staying with them at the

Ritz, a severe, bitter girl who loved Paula but was somewhat jealous of her impressive engagement, and as Paula was late in dressing, the cousin, who wasn't going to the party, received Anson in the parlour of the suite.

Anson had met friends at five o'clock and drunk freely and indiscreetly with them for an hour. He left the Yale Club at a proper time, and his mother's chauffeur drove him to the Ritz, but his usual capacity was not in evidence, and the impact of the steam-heated sitting-room made him suddenly dizzy. He knew it, and he was both amused and sorry.

Paula's cousin was twenty-five, but she was exceptionally naive, and at first failed to realise what was up. She had never met Anson before, and she was surprised when he mumbled strange information and nearly fell off his chair, but until Paula appeared it didn't occur to her that what she had taken for the odour of a dry-cleaned uniform was really whiskey. But Paula understood as soon as she appeared; her only thought was to get Anson away before her mother saw him, and at the look in her eyes the cousin understood too.

When Paula and Anson descended to the limousine they found two men inside, both asleep; they were the men with whom he had been drinking at the Yale Club, and they were also going to the party. He had entirely forgotten their presence in the car. On the way to Hempstead they awoke and sang. Some of the songs were rough, and though Paula tried to reconcile herself to the fact that Anson had few verbal inhibitions, her lips tightened with shame and distaste.

Back at the hotel the cousin, confused and agitated, considered the incident, and then walked into Mrs Legendre's bedroom, saying, 'Isn't he funny?'

'Who is funny?'

'Why – Mr Hunter. He seemed so funny.'

Mrs Legendre looked at her sharply.

'How is he funny?'

'Why, he said he was French. I didn't know he was French.'

'That's absurd. You must have misunderstood.' She smiled: 'It was a joke.'

The cousin shook her head stubbornly.

'No. He said he was brought up in France. He said he couldn't speak any English, and that's why he couldn't talk to me. And he couldn't!'

Mrs Legendre looked away with impatience just as the cousin added thoughtfully, 'Perhaps it was because he was so drunk,' and walked out of room.

This curious report was true, Anson, finding his voice thick and uncontrollable, had taken the unusual refuge of announcing that he spoke no English. Years afterwards he used to tell that part of the story, and he invariably communicated the uproarious laughter which the memory aroused in him.

Five times in the next hour Mrs Legendre tried to get Hempstead on the phone. When she succeeded, there was a ten-minute delay before she heard Paula's voice on the wire.

'Cousin Jo told me Anson was intoxicated.'

'Oh, no...'

'Oh yes, Cousin Jo says he was intoxicated. He told her he was French, and fell off his chair and behaved as if he was very intoxicated. I don't want you to come home with him.'

'Mother, he's all right! Please don't worry about –'

'But I do worry. I think it's dreadful. I want you to promise me not to come home with him.'

'I'll take care of it, Mother...'

'I don't want you to come home with him.'

'All right, Mother. Goodbye.'

'Be sure now, Paula. Ask someone to bring you.'

Deliberately Paula took the receiver from her ear and hung it up. Her face was flushed with helpless annoyance. Anson was stretched out asleep in a bedroom upstairs, while the dinner party below was proceeding lamely towards conclusion.

The hour's drive had sobered him somewhat – his arrival was merely hilarious – and Paula hoped that the evening was not spoiled after all, but two imprudent cocktails before dinner completed the disaster. He talked boisterously and somewhat offensively to the party at large for fifteen minutes, and then slid silently under the table, like a man in an old print – but, unlike an old print, it was rather horrible without being at all quaint. None of the young girls present remarked upon the incident – it seemed to merit only silence. His uncle and two other men carried him upstairs, and it was just after this that Paula was called to the phone.

An hour later Anson awoke in a fog of nervous agony, through which he perceived after a moment the figure of his Uncle Robert standing by the door.

'…I said are you better?'

'What?'

'Do you feel better, old man?'

'Terrible,' said Anson.

'I'm going to try you on another Bromo-Seltzer. If you can hold it down, it'll do you good to sleep.'

With an effort Anson slid his legs from the bed and stood up.

'I'm all right,' he said dully.

'Take it easy.'

'I thin' if you gave me a glassbrandy I could go downstairs.'

'Oh no –'

'Yes, that's the only thin'. I'm all right now… I suppose I'm in Dutch dow' there.'

'They know you're a little under the weather,' said his uncle deprecatingly. 'But don't worry about it. Schuyler didn't even get here. He passed away in the locker-room over at the Links.'

Indifferent to any opinion, except Paula's, Anson was nevertheless determined to save the debris of the evening, but when after a cold bath he made his appearance, most of the party had already left. Paula got up immediately to go home.

In the limousine the old serious dialogue began. She had known that he drank, she admitted, but she had never expected anything like this – it seemed to her that perhaps they were not suited to each other, after all. Their ideas about life were too different, and so forth. When she finished speaking, Anson spoke in turn, very soberly. Then Paula said she'd have to think it over; she wouldn't decide tonight; she was angry but she was terribly sorry. Nor would she let him come into the hotel with her, but just before she got out of the car she leant and kissed him unhappily on the cheek.

The next afternoon Anson had a long talk with Mrs Legendre while Paula sat listening in silence. It was agreed that Paula was to brood over the incident for a proper period and then, if mother and daughter thought it best, they would follow Anson to Pensacola. On his part he apologised with sincerity and dignity – that was all; with every card in her hand, Mrs Legendre was unable to establish any advantage over him. He made no promises, showed no humility, only delivered a few serious comments on life which brought him off with rather a moral superiority at the end. When they came South three weeks later, neither Anson in his satisfaction nor Paula in her relief at the reunion realised that the psychological moment had passed for ever.

## 4

He dominated and attracted her, and at the same time filled her with anxiety. Confused by his mixture of solidity and self-indulgence, of sentiment and cynicism – incongruities which her gentle mind was unable to resolve – Paula grew to think of him as two alternating personalities. When she saw him alone, or at a formal party, or with his casual inferiors, she felt a tremendous pride in his strong, attractive presence, the paternal, understanding stature of his mind. In other company she became uneasy when what had been a fine imperviousness to mere gentility showed its other face. The other face was gross, humorous, reckless of everything but pleasure. It startled her mind temporarily away from him, even led her into a short, covert experiment with an old beau, but it was no use – after four months of Anson's enveloping vitality there was an anaemic pallor in all other men.

In July he was ordered abroad, and their tenderness and desire reached a crescendo. Paula considered a last-minute marriage – decided against it only because there were always cocktails on his breath now, but the parting itself made her physically ill with grief. After his departure she wrote him long letters of regret for the days of love they had missed by waiting. In August Anson's plane slipped down into the North Sea. He was pulled onto a destroyer after a night in the water and sent to hospital with pneumonia; the armistice was signed before he was finally sent home.

Then, with every opportunity given back to them, with no material obstacle to overcome, the secret weavings of their temperaments came between them, drying up their kisses and their tears, making their voices less loud to one another, muffling the intimate chatter of their hearts until the old communication was only possible by letters, from far away. One afternoon a society reporter waited for two hours in the Hunters' house for a confirmation of their engagement. Anson denied it; nevertheless an early issue carried the report as a leading paragraph – they were 'constantly seen together at Southampton, Hot Springs, and Tuxedo Park'. But the serious dialogue had turned a corner into a long-sustained quarrel, and the affair was almost played out. Anson got drunk flagrantly and missed an engagement with her, whereupon Paula made certain behaviouristic demands. His despair was helpless before his pride and his knowledge of himself: the engagement was definitely broken.

'Dearest,' said their letters now, 'Dearest, Dearest, when I wake up in the middle of the night and realise that after all it was not to be, I feel that I want to die. I can't go on living any more. Perhaps when we meet this summer we may talk things over and decide differently – we were so excited and sad that day, and I don't feel that I can live all my life without you. You speak of other people. Don't you know there are no other people for me, but only you…'

But as Paula drifted here and there around the East she would sometimes mention her gaieties to make him wonder. Anson was too acute to wonder. When he saw a man's name in her letters he felt more sure of her and a little disdainful – he was always superior to such things. But he still hoped that they would some day marry.

Meanwhile he plunged vigorously into all the movement and glitter of post-bellum New York, entering a brokerage house, joining half a dozen clubs, dancing late, and moving in three worlds – his own world, the world of young Yale graduates, and that section of the half-world which rests one end on Broadway. But there was always a thorough and infractible eight hours devoted to his work in Wall Street, where the combination of his influential family connection, his sharp intelligence, and his abundance of sheer physical energy brought him almost immediately forward. He had one of those invaluable minds with partitions in it; sometimes he appeared at his office refreshed by less than an hour's sleep, but such occurrences were rare. So early as 1920 his income in salary and commissions exceeded twelve thousand dollars.

As the Yale tradition slipped into the past he became more and more of a popular figure among his classmates in New York, more popular than he had ever been in college. He lived in a great house, and had the means of introducing young men into other great houses. Moreover, his life already seemed secure, while theirs, for the most part, had arrived again at precarious beginnings. They commenced to turn to him for amusement and escape, and Anson responded readily, taking pleasure in helping people and arranging their affairs.

There were no men in Paula's letters now, but a note of tenderness ran through them that had not been there before. From several sources he heard that she had 'a heavy beau', Lowell Thayer, a Bostonian of wealth and position, and though he was sure she still loved him, it made him uneasy to think that he might lose her, after all. Save for one unsatisfactory day she had not been in New York for almost five months, and as the rumours multiplied he became increasingly anxious to see her. In February he took his vacation and went down to Florida.

Palm Beach sprawled plump and opulent between the sparkling sapphire of Lake Worth, flawed here and there by houseboats at anchor, and the great turquoise bar of the Atlantic Ocean. The huge bulks of the Breakers and the Royal Poinciana rose as twin paunches from the bright level of the sand, and around them clustered the Dancing Glade, Bradley's House of Chance, and a dozen modistes and milliners with goods at triple prices from New York. Upon the trellised veranda of the Breakers two hundred women stepped right, stepped left, wheeled, and slid in that then celebrated callisthenic known as the double shuffle, while in half-time to the music two thousand bracelets clicked up and down on two hundred arms.

At the Everglades Club after dark Paula and Lowell Thayer and Anson and a casual fourth played bridge with hot cards. It seemed to Anson that her kind, serious face was wan and tired – she had been around now for four, five years. He had known her for three.

'Two spades.'

'Cigarette?… Oh, I beg your pardon. By me.'

'By.'

'I'll double three spades.'

There were a dozen tables of bridge in the room, which was filling up with smoke. Anson's eyes met Paula's, held them persistently even when Thayer's glance fell between them…

'What was bid?' he asked abstractedly.

'Rose of Washington Square'

sang the young people in the corners:

'I'm withering there
In basement air…'

The smoke banked like fog, and the opening of a door filled the room with blown swirls of ectoplasm. Little Bright Eyes streaked past the tables seeking Mr Conan Doyle among the

Englishmen who were posing as Englishmen about the lobby.

'You could cut it with a knife.'

'…cut it with a knife.'

'…a knife.'

At the end of the rubber Paula suddenly got up and spoke to Anson in a tense, low voice. With scarcely a glance at Lowell Thayer, they walked out the door and descended a long flight of stone steps – in a moment they were walking hand in hand along the moonlit beach.

'Darling, darling…' They embraced recklessly, passionately, in a shadow… Then Paula drew back her face to let his lips say what she wanted to hear – she could feel the words forming as they kissed again… Again she broke away, listening, but as he pulled her close once more she realised that he had said nothing – only *'Darling! Darling!'* in that deep, sad whisper that always made her cry. Humbly, obediently, her emotions yielded to him and the tears streamed down her face, but her heart kept on crying, 'Ask me – oh, Anson, ask me!'

'Paula… *Paula!'*

The words wrung her heart like hands, and Anson, feeling her tremble, knew that emotion was enough. He need say no more, commit their destinies to no practical enigma. Why should he, when he might hold her so, biding his own time, for another year – for ever? He was considering them both, her more than himself. For a moment, when she said suddenly that she must go back to her hotel, he hesitated, thinking first, 'This is the moment, after all,' and then, 'No, let it wait – she is mine…'

He had forgotten that Paula too was worn away inside with the strain of three years. Her mood passed for ever in the night.

He went back to New York next morning filled with a

certain restless dissatisfaction. Late in April, without warning, he received a telegram from Bar Harbour in which Paula told him that she was engaged to Lowell Thayer, and that they would be married immediately in Boston. What he never really believed could happen had happened at last.

Anson filled himself with whiskey that morning, and going to the office, carried on his work without a break – rather with a fear of what would happen if he stopped. In the evening he went out as usual, saying nothing of what had occurred; he was cordial, humorous, unabstracted. But one thing he could not help – for three days, in any place, in any company, he would suddenly bend his head into his hands and cry like a child.

## 5

In 1922 when Anson went abroad with the junior partner to investigate some London loans, the journey intimated that he was to be taken into the firm. He was twenty-seven now, a little heavy without being definitely stout, and with a manner older than his years. Old people and young people liked him and trusted him, and mothers felt safe when their daughters were in his charge, for he had a way, when he came into a room, of putting himself on a footing with the oldest and most conservative people there. 'You and I,' he seemed to say, 'we're solid. We understand.'

He had an instinctive and rather charitable knowledge of the weaknesses of men and women, and, like a priest, it made him the more concerned for the maintenance of outward forms. It was typical of him that every Sunday morning he taught in a fashionable Episcopal Sunday school – even though a cold shower and a quick change into a cut-away coat were all that separated him from the wild night before.

After his father's death he was the practical head of his family, and, in effect, guided the destinies of the younger children. Through a complication, his authority did not extend to his father's estate, which was administered by his Uncle Robert, who was the horsey member of the family, a good-natured, hard-drinking member of that set which centres about Wheatley Hills.

Uncle Robert and his wife, Edna, had been great friends of Anson's youth, and the former was disappointed when his nephew's superiority failed to take a horsey form. He backed him for a city club which was the most difficult in America to enter – one could only join if one's family had 'helped to build up New York' (or, in other words, were rich before 1880) – and when Anson, after his election, neglected it for the Yale Club, Uncle Robert gave him a little talk on the subject. But when on top of that Anson declined to enter Robert Hunter's own conservative and somewhat neglected brokerage house, his manner grew cooler. Like a primary teacher who has taught all he knew, he slipped out of Anson's life.

There were so many friends in Anson's life – scarcely one for whom he had not done some unusual kindness and scarcely one whom he did not occasionally embarrass by his bursts of rough conversation or his habit of getting drunk whenever and however he liked. It annoyed him when anyone else blundered in that regard – about his own lapses he was always humorous. Odd things happened to him and he told them with infectious laughter.

I was working in New York that spring, and I used to lunch with him at the Yale Club, which my university was sharing until the completion of our own. I had read of

Paula's marriage, and one afternoon, when I asked him about her, something moved him to tell me the story. After that he frequently invited me to family dinners at his house and behaved as though there was a special relation between us, as though with his confidence a little of that consuming memory had passed into me.

I found that despite the trusting mothers, his attitude towards girls was not indiscriminately protective. It was up to the girl – if she showed an inclination towards looseness, she must take care of herself, even with him.

'Life,' he would explain sometimes, 'has made a cynic of me.'

By life he meant Paula. Sometimes, especially when he was drinking, it became a little twisted in his mind, and he thought that she had callously thrown him over.

This 'cynicism', or rather his realisation that naturally fast girls were not worth sparing, led to his affair with Dolly Karger. It wasn't his only affair in those years, but it came nearest to touching him deeply, and it had a profound effect upon his attitude towards life.

Dolly was the daughter of a notorious 'publicist' who had married into society. She herself grew up into the Junior League, came out at the Plaza, and went to the Assembly; and only a few old families like the Hunters could question whether or not she 'belonged', for her picture was often in the papers, and she had more enviable attention than many girls who undoubtedly did. She was dark-haired, with carmine lips and a high, lovely colour, which she concealed under pinkish-grey powder all through the first year out, because high colour was unfashionable – Victorian-pale was the thing to be. She wore black, severe suits, and stood with her hands in her pockets leaning a little forward, with a humorous restraint on her face. She danced exquisitely – better than anything she liked to dance – better than anything except making love. Since she was ten she had always been in love, and, usually, with some boy who didn't respond to her. Those who did – and there were many – bored her after a brief encounter, but for her failures she reserved the warmest spot in her heart. When she met them she would always try once more – sometimes she succeeded, more often she failed.

It never occurred to this gypsy of the unattainable that there was a certain resemblance in those who refused to love her – they shared a hard intuition that saw through to her weakness, not a weakness of emotion but a weakness of rudder. Anson perceived this when he first met her, less than a month after Paula's marriage. He was drinking rather heavily, and he pretended for a week that he was falling in love with her. Then he dropped her abruptly and forgot – immediately he took up the commanding position in her heart.

Like so many girls of that day Dolly was slackly and indiscreetly wild. The unconventionality of a slightly older generation had been simply one facet of a post-war movement to discredit obsolete manners – Dolly's was both older and shabbier, and she saw in Anson the two extremes which the emotionally shiftless woman seeks, an abandon to indulgence alternating with a protective strength. In his character she felt both the sybarite and the solid rock, and these two satisfied every need of her nature.

She felt that it was going to be difficult, but she mistook the reason – she thought that Anson and his family expected a more spectacular marriage, but she guessed immediately that her advantage lay in his tendency to drink.

They met at the large debutante dances, but as her infatuation increased they managed to be more and more together. Like most mothers, Mrs Karger believed that Anson was exceptionally reliable, so she allowed Dolly to go with him to distant country clubs and suburban houses without enquiring closely into their activities or questioning her explanations when they came in late. At first these explanations might have been accurate, bur Dolly's worldly ideas of capturing Anson were soon engulfed in the rising sweep of her emotion. Kisses in the back of taxis and motor cars were no longer enough; they did a curious thing:

They dropped out of their world for a while and made another world just beneath it where Anson's tippling and Dolly's irregular hours would be less noticed and commented on. It was composed, this world, of varying elements – several of Anson's Yale friends and their wives, two or three young brokers and bond salesmen, and a handful of unattached men, fresh from college, with money and a propensity to dissipation. What this world lacked in spaciousness and scale it made up for by allowing them a liberty that it scarcely permitted itself. Moreover, it centred around them and permitted Dolly the pleasure of a faint condescension – a pleasure which Anson, whose whole life was a condescension from the certitudes of his childhood, was unable to share.

He was not in love with her, and in the long feverish winter of their affair he frequently told her so. In the spring he was weary – he wanted to renew his life at some other source – moreover, he saw that either he must break with her now or accept the responsibility of a definite seduction. Her family's encouraging attitude precipitated his decision – one evening when Mr Karger knocked discreetly at the library door to announce that he had left a bottle of old brandy in the dining-room, Anson felt that life was hemming him in. That night he wrote her a short letter in which he told her that he was going on his vacation, and that in view of all the circumstances they had better meet no more.

It was June. His family had closed up the house and gone to the country, so he was living temporarily at the Yale Club. I had heard about his affair with Dolly as it developed – accounts salted with humour, for he despised unstable women, and granted them no place in the social edifice in which he believed – and when he told me that night that he was definitely breaking with her I was glad. I had seen Dolly here and there, and each time with a feeling of pity at the hopelessness of her struggle, and of shame at knowing so much about her that I had no right to know. She was what is known as 'a pretty little thing', but there was a certain recklessness which rather fascinated me. Her dedication to the goddess of waste would have been less obvious had she been less spirited – she would most certainly throw herself away, but I was glad when I heard that the sacrifice would not be consummated in my sight.

Anson was going to leave the letter of farewell at her house next morning. It was one of the few houses left open in the Fifth Avenue district, and he knew that the Kargers, acting upon erroneous information from Dolly, had foregone a trip abroad to give their daughter her chance. As he stepped out the door of the Yale Club into Madison Avenue the postman passed him, and he followed back inside. The first letter that caught his eye was in Dolly's hand.

He knew what it would be – a lonely and tragic monologue, full of the reproaches he knew, the invoked memories, and 'I wonder ifs' – all the immemorial intimacies that he had communicated to Paula Legendre in what seemed another age. Thumbing over some bills, he brought it on top again and opened it. To his surprise it was a short, somewhat formal note, which said that Dolly would be unable to go to the country with him for the weekend, because Perry Hull from Chicago had unexpectedly come to town. It added that Anson had brought this on himself: '– if I felt that you loved me as I love you I would go with you at any time, any place, but Perry is *so* nice, and he so much wants me to marry him –'

Anson smiled contemptuously – he had had experience with such decoy epistles. Moreover, he knew how Dolly had laboured over this plan, probably sent for the faithful Perry and calculated the time of his arrival – even laboured over the note so that it would make him jealous without driving him away. Like most compromises, it had neither force nor vitality but only a timorous despair.

Suddenly he was angry. He sat down in the lobby and read it again. Then he went to the phone, called Dolly and told her in his clear, compelling voice that he had received her note and would call for her at five o'clock as they had previously planned. Scarcely waiting for the pretended uncertainty of her 'Perhaps I can see you for an hour', he hung up the receiver and went down to his office. On the way he tore his own letter into bits and dropped it in the street.

He was not jealous – she meant nothing to him – but at her pathetic ruse everything stubborn and self-indulgent in him came to the surface. It was a presumption from a mental inferior and it could not be overlooked. If she wanted to know to whom she belonged she would see.

He was on the doorstep at quarter-past five. Dolly was dressed for the street, and he listened in silence to the paragraph of 'I can only see you for an hour', which she had begun on the phone.

'Put on your hat, Dolly,' he said, 'we'll take a walk.'

They strolled up Madison Avenue and over to Fifth while Anson's shirt dampened upon his portly body in the deep heat. He talked little, scolding her, making no love to her, but before they had walked six blocks she was his again, apologising for the note, offering not to see Perry at all as an atonement, offering anything. She thought that he had come because he was beginning to love her.

'I'm hot,' he said when they reached 71st Street. 'This is a winter suit. If I stop by the house and change, would you mind waiting for me downstairs? I'll only be a minute.'

She was happy; the intimacy of his being hot, of any physical fact about him, thrilled her. When they came to the iron-grated door and Anson took out his key she experienced a sort of delight.

Downstairs it was dark, and after he ascended in the lift Dolly raised a curtain and looked out through opaque lace at the houses over the way. She heard the lift machinery stop, and with the notion of teasing him pressed the button that brought it down. Then on what was more than an impulse she got into it and sent it up to what she guessed was his floor.

'Anson,' she called, laughing a little.

'Just a minute,' he answered from his bedroom… then after a brief delay: 'Now you can come in.'

He had changed and was buttoning his vest.

'This is my room,' he said lightly. 'How do you like it?'

She caught sight of Paula's picture on the wall and stared at it in fascination, just as Paula had stared at the pictures of Anson's childish sweethearts five years before. She knew something about Paula – sometimes she tortured herself with fragments of the story.

Suddenly she came close to Anson, raising her arms. They embraced. Outside the area window a soft artificial twilight already hovered, though the sun was still bright on a back roof across the way. In half an hour the room would be quite dark. The uncalculated opportunity overwhelmed them, made them both breathless, and they clung more closely. It was imminent, inevitable. Still holding one another, they raised their heads – their eyes fell together upon Paula's picture, staring down at them from the wall.

Suddenly Anson dropped his arms, and sitting down at his desk tried the drawer with a bunch of keys.

'Like a drink?' he asked in a gruff voice.

'No, Anson.'

He poured himself half a tumbler of whiskey, swallowed it, and then opened the door into the hall.

'Come on,' he said.

Dolly hesitated.

'Anson – I'm going to the country with you tonight, after all. You understand that, don't you?'

'Of course,' he answered brusquely.

In Dolly's car they rode on to Long Island, closer in their emotions than they had ever been before. They knew what would happen – not with Paula's face to remind them that something was lacking, but when they were alone in the still, hot Long Island night they did not care.

The estate in Port Washington where they were to spend the weekend belonged to a cousin of Anson's who had married a Montana copper operator. An interminable drive began at the lodge and twisted under imported poplar saplings towards a huge, pink Spanish house. Anson had often visited there before.

After dinner they danced at the Linx Club. About midnight Anson assured himself that his cousins would not leave before two – then he explained that Dolly was tired; he would take

26

her home and return to the dance later. Trembling a little with excitement, they got into a borrowed car together and drove to Port Washington. As they reached the lodge he stopped and spoke to the nightwatchman.

'When are you making a round, Carl?'

'Right away.'

'Then you'll be here till everybody's in?'

'Yes, sir.'

'All right. Listen: if any automobile, no matter whose it is, turns in a gate, I want you to phone the house immediately.' He put a five-dollar bill into Carl's hand.

'Is that clear?'

'Yes, Mr Anson.' Being of the Old World, he neither winked nor smiled. Yet Dolly sat with her face turned slightly away.

Anson had a key. Once inside he poured a drink for both of them – Dolly left hers untouched – then he ascertained definitely the location of the phone, and found that it was within easy hearing distance of their rooms, both of which were on the first floor.

Five minutes later he knocked at the door of Dolly's room.

'Anson?' He went in, closing the door behind him. She was in bed, leaning up anxiously with elbows on the pillow; sitting beside her he took her in his arms.

'Anson, darling.'

He didn't answer.

'Anson... Anson! I love you... Say you love me. Say it now – can't you say it now? Even if you don't mean it?'

He did not listen. Over her head he perceived that the picture of Paula was hanging here upon this wall.

He got up and went close to it. The frame gleamed faintly with thrice-reflected moonlight – within was a blurred shadow of a face that he saw he did not know. Almost sobbing, he turned around and stared with abomination at the little figure on the bed.

'This is all foolishness,' he said thickly. 'I don't know what I was thinking about. I don't love you and you'd better wait for somebody that loves you. I don't love you a bit, can't you understand?'

His voice broke, and he went hurriedly out. Back in the saloon he was pouring himself a drink with uneasy fingers, when the front door opened suddenly, and his cousin came in.

'Why, Anson, I hear Dolly's sick,' she began solicitously. 'I hear she's sick…'

'It was nothing,' he interrupted, raising his voice so that it would carry into Dolly's room. 'She was a little tired. She went to bed.'

For a long time afterwards Anson believed that a protective God sometimes interfered in human affairs. But Dolly Karger, lying awake and staring at the ceiling, never again believed in anything at all.

6

When Dolly married during the following autumn, Anson was in London on business. Like Paula's marriage, it was sudden, but it affected him in a different way. At first he felt that it was funny, and had an inclination to laugh when he thought of it. Later it depressed him – it made him feel old.

There was something repetitive about it – why, Paula and Dolly had belonged to different generations. He had a foretaste of the sensation of a man of forty who hears that the daughter of an old flame has married. He wired congratulations and, as was not the case with Paula, they were sincere – he had never really hoped that Paula would be happy.

When he returned to New York, he was made a partner in the firm, and, as his responsibilities increased, he had less time on his hands. The refusal of a life-insurance company to issue him a policy made such an impression on him that he stopped drinking for a year, and claimed that he felt better physically, though I think he missed the convivial recounting of those Celliniesque adventures which, in his early twenties, had played such a part in his life. But he never abandoned the Yale Club. He was a figure there, a personality, and the tendency of his class, who were now seven years out of college, to drift away to more sober haunts was checked by his presence.

His day was never too full nor his mind too weary to give any sort of aid to anyone who asked it. What had been done at first through pride and superiority had become a habit and passion. And there was always something – a younger brother in trouble at New Haven, a quarrel to be patched up between a friend and his wife, a position to be found for this man, an investment for that. But his speciality was the solving of problems for young married people. Young married people fascinated him and their apartments were almost sacred to him – he knew the story of their love affair, advised them where to live and how, and remembered their babies' names. Towards young wives his attitude was circumspect: he never abused the trust which their husbands – strangely enough in view of his unconcealed irregularities – invariably reposed in him.

He came to take a vicarious pleasure in happy marriages, and to be inspired to an almost equally pleasant melancholy by those that went astray. Not a season passed that he did not witness the collapse of an affair that perhaps he himself had fathered. When Paula was divorced and almost immediately remarried to another Bostonian, he talked about her to me all one afternoon. He would never love anyone as he had loved Paula, but he insisted that he no longer cared.

'I'll never marry,' he came to say; 'I've seen too much of it, and I know a happy marriage is a very rare thing. Besides, I'm too old.'

But he did believe in marriage. Like all men who spring from a happy and successful marriage, he believed in it passionately – nothing he had seen would change his belief, his cynicism dissolved upon it like air. But he did really believe he was too old. At twenty-eight he began to accept with equanimity the prospect of marrying without romantic love; he resolutely chose a New York girl of his own class, pretty, intelligent, congenial, above reproach – and set about falling in love with her. The things he had said to Paula with sincerity, to other girls with grace, he could no longer say at all without smiling, or with the force necessary to convince.

'When I'm forty,' he told his friends, 'I'll be ripe. I'll fall for some chorus girl like the rest.'

Nevertheless, he persisted in his attempt. His mother wanted to see him married, and he could now well afford it – he had a seat on the Stock Exchange, and his earned income came to twenty-five thousand a year. The idea was agreeable: when his friends – he spent most of his time with the set he and Dolly had evolved – closed themselves in behind domestic doors at night, he no longer rejoiced in his freedom. He even wondered if he should have married Dolly. Not even Paula had loved him more, and he was learning the rarity, in a single life, of encountering true emotion.

Just as this mood began to creep over him a disquieting story reached his ear. His Aunt Edna, a woman just this side of forty, was carrying on an open intrigue with a dissolute, hard-drinking young man named Cary Sloane. Everyone knew of it except Anson's Uncle Robert, who for fifteen years had talked long in clubs and taken his wife for granted.

Anson heard the story again and again with increasing annoyance. Something of his old feeling for his uncle came back to him, a feeling that was more than personal, a reversion towards that family solidarity on which he had based his pride. His intuition singled out the essential point of the affair, which was that his uncle shouldn't be hurt. It was his first experiment in unsolicited meddling, but with his knowledge of Edna's character he felt that he could handle the matter better than a district judge or his uncle.

His uncle was in Hot Springs. Anson traced down the sources of the scandal so that there should be no possibility of mistake and then he called Edna and asked her to lunch with him at the Plaza next day. Something in his tone must have frightened her, for she was reluctant, but he insisted, putting off the date until she had no excuse for refusing.

She met him at the appointed time in the Plaza lobby, a lovely, faded, grey-eyed blonde in a coat of Russian sable. Five great rings, cold with diamonds and emeralds, sparkled on her slender hands. It occurred to Anson that it was his father's intelligence and not his uncle's that had earned the fur and the stones, the rich brilliance that buoyed up her passing beauty.

Though Edna scented his hostility, she was unprepared for the directness of his approach.

'Edna, I'm astonished at the way you've been acting,' he said in a strong, frank voice. 'At first I couldn't believe it.'

'Believe what?' she demanded sharply.

'You needn't pretend with me, Edna. I'm talking about Cary Sloane. Aside from any other consideration, I didn't think you could treat Uncle Robert –'

'Now look here, Anson –' she began angrily, but his peremptory voice broke through hers:

'– and your children in such a way. You've been married eighteen years, and you're old enough to know better.'

'You can't talk to me like that! You –'

'Yes, I can. Uncle Robert has always been my best friend.' He was tremendously moved. He felt a real distress about his uncle, about his three young cousins.

Edna stood up, leaving her crab-flake cocktail untasted.

'This is the silliest thing –'

'Very well, if you won't listen to me I'll go to Uncle Robert and tell him the whole story – he's bound to hear it sooner or later. And afterward I'll go to old Moses Sloane.'

Edna faltered back into her chair.

'Don't talk so loud,' she begged him. Her eyes blurred with tears. 'You have no idea how your voice carries. You might have chosen a less public place to make all these crazy accusations.'

He didn't answer.

'Oh, you never liked me, I know,' she went on. 'You're just taking advantage of some silly gossip to try and break up the only interesting friendship I've ever had. What did I ever do to make you hate me so?'

Still Anson waited. There would be the appeal to his chivalry, then to his pity, finally to his superior sophistication – when he had shouldered his way through all these there would be admissions, and he could come to grips with her. By being silent, by being impervious, by returning constantly to his main weapon, which was his own true emotion, he bullied her into frantic despair as the luncheon hour slipped away. At two o'clock she took out a mirror and a handkerchief, shined away

32

the marks of her tears and powdered the slight hollows where they had lain. She had agreed to meet him at her own house at five.

When he arrived she was stretched on a chaise longue which was covered with cretonne for the summer, and the tears he had called up at luncheon seemed still to be standing in her eyes. Then he was aware of Cary Sloane's dark, anxious presence upon the cold hearth.

'What's this idea of yours?' broke out Sloane immediately. 'I understand you invited Edna to lunch and then threatened her on the basis of some cheap scandal.'

Anson sat down.

'I have no reason to think it's only scandal.'

'I hear you're going to take it to Robert Hunter, and to my father.'

Anson nodded.

'Either you break it off – or I will,' he said.

'What goddamned business is it of yours, Hunter?'

'Don't lose your temper, Cary,' said Edna nervously. 'It's only a question of showing him how absurd –'

'For one thing, it's my name that's being handed around,' interrupted Anson. 'That's all that concerns you, Cary.'

'Edna isn't a member of your family.'

'She most certainly is!' His anger mounted. 'Why – she owes this house and the rings on her fingers to my father's brains. When Uncle Robert married her she didn't have a penny.'

They all looked at the rings as if they had a significant bearing on the situation. Edna made a gesture to take them from her hand.

'I guess they're not the only rings in the world,' said Sloane.

'Oh, this is absurd,' cried Edna. 'Anson, will you listen to me? I've found out how the silly story started. It was a maid I discharged who went right to the Chilicheffs – all these Russians pump things out of their servants and then put a false meaning on them.' She brought down her fist angrily on the table: 'And after Robert lent them the limousine for a whole month when we were South last winter –'

'Do you see?' demanded Sloane eagerly. 'This maid got hold of the wrong end of the thing. She knew that Edna and I were friends, and she carried it to the Chilicheffs. In Russia they assume that if a man and a woman…'

He enlarged the theme to a disquisition upon social relations in the Caucasus.

'If that's the case it better be explained to Uncle Robert,' said Anson dryly, 'so that when the rumours do reach him he'll know they're not true.'

Adopting the method he had followed with Edna at luncheon he let them explain it all away. He knew that they were guilty and that presently they would cross the line from explanation into justification and convict themselves more definitely than he could ever do. By seven they had taken the desperate step of telling him the truth – Robert Hunter's neglect, Edna's empty life, the casual dalliance that had flamed up into passion – but like so many true stories it had the misfortune of being old, and its enfeebled body beat helplessly against the armour of Anson's will. The threat to go to Sloane's father sealed their helplessness, for the latter, a retired cotton broker out of Alabama, was a notorious fundamentalist who controlled his son by a rigid allowance and the promise that at his next vagary the allowance would stop for ever.

They dined at a small French restaurant, and the discussion continued – at one time Sloane resorted to physical threats, a little later they were both imploring him to give them time. But

Anson was obdurate. He saw that Edna was breaking up, and that her spirit must not be refreshed by any renewal of their passion.

At two o'clock in a small nightclub on 53rd Street, Edna's nerves suddenly collapsed, and she cried to go home. Sloane had been drinking heavily all evening, and he was faintly maudlin, leaning on the table and weeping a little with his face in his hands. Quickly Anson gave them his terms. Sloane was to leave town for six months, and he must be gone within forty-eight hours. When he returned there was to be no resumption of the affair, but at the end of a year Edna might, if she wished, tell Robert Hunter that she wanted a divorce and go about it in the usual way.

He paused, gaining confidence from their faces for his final word.

'Or there's another thing you can do,' he said slowly, 'if Edna wants to leave her children, there's nothing I can do to prevent your running off together.'

'I want to go home!' cried Edna again. 'Oh, haven't you done enough to us for one day?'

Outside it was dark, save for a blurred glow from Sixth Avenue down the street. In that light those two who had been lovers looked for the last time into each other's tragic faces, realising that between them there was not enough youth and strength to avert their eternal parting. Sloane walked suddenly off down the street and Anson tapped a dozing taxi-driver on the arm.

It was almost four; there was a patient flow of cleaning water along the ghostly pavement of Fifth Avenue, and the shadows of two night-women flitted over the dark façade of St Thomas' church. Then the desolate shrubbery of Central Park where Anson had often played as a child, and the mounting numbers, significant as names, of the marching streets. This was his city, he thought, where his name had flourished through five generations. No change could alter the permanence of its place here, for change itself was the essential substratum by which he and those of his name identified themselves with the spirit of New York. Resourcefulness and a powerful will – for his threats in weaker hands would have been less than nothing – had beaten the gathering dust from his uncle's name, from the name of his family, from even this shivering figure that sat beside him in the car.

Cary Sloane's body was found next morning on the lower shelf of a pillar of Queensboro Bridge. In the darkness and in his excitement he had thought that it was the water flowing black beneath him, but in less than a second it made no possible difference – unless he had planned to think one last thought of Edna, and call out her name as he struggled feebly in the water.


7


Anson never blamed himself for his part in this affair – the situation which brought it about had not been of his making. But the just suffer with the unjust, and he found that his oldest and somehow his most precious friendship was over. He never knew what distorted story Edna told, but he was welcome in his uncle's house no longer.

Just before Christmas Mrs Hunter retired to a select Episcopal heaven, and Anson became the responsible head of his family. An unmarried aunt who had lived with them for years ran the house, and attempted with helpless inefficiency to chaperone the younger girls. All the children were less self-reliant than Anson, more conventional both in their virtues and in their shortcomings. Mrs Hunter's death had postponed the debut of one daughter and the wedding of another. Also it had taken something deeply material from all of them, for with her passing the quiet, expensive superiority of the Hunters came to an end.

For one thing, the estate, considerably diminished by two inheritance taxes and soon to be divided among six children, was not a notable fortune any more. Anson saw a tendency in his youngest sisters to speak rather respectfully of families that hadn't 'existed' twenty years ago. His own feeling of precedence was not echoed in them – sometimes they were conventionally snobbish, that was all. For another thing, this was the last summer they would spend on the Connecticut estate; the clamour against it was too loud: 'Who wants to waste the best months of the year shut up in that dead old town?' Reluctantly he yielded – the house would go into the market in the fall, and next summer they would rent a smaller place in Westchester County. It was a step down from the expensive simplicity of his father's idea, and, while he sympathised with the revolt, it also annoyed him; during his mother's lifetime he had gone up there at least every other weekend – even in the gayest summers.

Yet he himself was part of this change, and his strong instinct for life had turned him in his twenties from the hollow obsequies of that abortive leisure class. He did not see this clearly – he still felt that there was a norm, a standard of society. But there was no norm, it was doubtful if there ever had been a true norm in New York. The few who still paid and fought to enter a particular set succeeded only to find that as a society it scarcely functioned – or, what was more alarming, that the Bohemia from which they fled sat above them at table.

At twenty-nine Anson's chief concern was his own growing loneliness. He was sure now that he would never marry. The number of weddings at which he had officiated as best man or usher was past all counting – there was a drawer at home that bulged with the official neckties of this or that wedding party, neckties standing for romances that had not endured a year, for couples who had passed completely from his life. Scarf-pins, gold pencils, cuff-buttons, presents from a generation of grooms had passed through his jewel box and been lost – and with every ceremony he was less and less able to imagine himself in the groom's place. Under his hearty goodwill towards all those marriages there was despair about his own.

And as he neared thirty he became not a little depressed at the inroads that marriage, especially lately, had made upon his friendships. Groups of people had a disconcerting tendency to dissolve and disappear. The men from his own college – and it was upon them he had expended the most time and affection – were the most elusive of all. Most of them were drawn deep into domesticity, two were dead, one lived abroad, one was in Hollywood writing continuities for pictures that Anson went faithfully to see.

Most of them, however, were permanent commuters with an intricate family life centring around some suburban country club, and it was from these that he felt his estrangement most keenly.

In the early days of their married life they had all needed him; he gave them advice about their slim finances, he exorcised their doubts about the advisability of bringing a baby into two rooms and a bath, especially he stood for the great world outside. But now their financial troubles were in the past and the fearfully expected child had evolved into an absorbing family. They were always glad to see old Anson, but they dressed up for him and tried to impress him with their present importance, and kept their troubles to themselves. They needed him no longer.

A few weeks before his thirtieth birthday the last of his early and intimate friends was married. Anson acted in his usual role of best man, gave his usual silver tea-service, and went down to the usual *Homeric* to say goodbye. It was a hot Friday afternoon in May, and as he walked from the pier he realised that Saturday closing had begun and he was free until Monday morning.

'Go where?' he asked himself.

The Yale Club, of course; bridge until dinner, then four or five raw cocktails in somebody's room and a pleasant confused evening. He regretted that this afternoon's groom wouldn't be along – they had always been able to cram so much into such nights: they knew how to attach women and how to get rid of them, how much consideration any girl deserved from their intelligent hedonism. A party was an adjusted thing – you took certain girls to certain places and spent just so much on their amusement; you drank a little, not much, more than you ought to drink, and at a certain time in the morning you stood up and said you were going home. You avoided college boys, sponges, future engagements, fights, sentiment, and indiscretions. That was the way it was done. All the rest was dissipation.

In the morning you were never violently sorry – you made no resolutions, but if you had overdone it and your heart was slightly out of order, you went on the wagon for a few days without saying anything about it, and waited until an accumulation of nervous boredom projected you into another party.

The lobby of the Yale Club was unpopulated. In the bar three very young alumni looked up at him, momentarily and without curiosity.

'Hello, there, Oscar,' he said to the bartender. 'Mr Cahill been around this afternoon?'

'Mr Cahill's gone to New Haven.'

'Oh… that so?'

'Gone to the ball game. Lot of men gone up.'

Anson looked once again into the lobby, considered for a moment, and then walked out and over to Fifth Avenue. From the broad window of one of his clubs – one that he had scarcely visited in five years – a grey man with watery eyes stared down at him. Anson looked quickly away – that figure sitting in vacant resignation, in supercilious solitude, depressed him. He stopped and, retracing his steps, started over 47th Street towards Teak Warden's apartment. Teak and his wife had once been his most familiar friends – it was a household where he and Dolly Karger had been used to go in the days of their affair. But Teak had taken to drink, and his wife had remarked publicly that Anson was a bad influence on him. The remark reached Anson in an exaggerated form – when it was finally cleared up, the delicate spell of intimacy was broken, never to be renewed.

'Is Mr Warden at home?' he enquired.

'They've gone to the country.'

The fact unexpectedly cut at him. They were gone to the country and he hadn't known. Two years before he would have known the date, the hour, come up at the last moment for a final drink, and planned his first visit to them. Now they had gone without a word.

Anson looked at this watch and considered a weekend with his family, but the only train was a local that would jolt through the aggressive heat for three hours. And tomorrow in the country, and Sunday – he was in no mood for porch-bridge with polite undergraduates, and dancing after dinner at a rural roadhouse, a diminutive of gaiety which his father had estimated too well.

'Oh, no,' he said to himself… 'No.'

He was a dignified, impressive young man, rather stout now, but otherwise unmarked by dissipation. He could have been cast for a pillar of something – at times you were sure it was not society, at others nothing else – for the law, for the Church. He stood for a few minutes motionless on the sidewalk in front of a 47th Street apartment house; for almost the first time in his life he had nothing whatever to do.

Then he began to walk briskly up Fifth Avenue, as if he had just been reminded of an important engagement there. The necessity of dissimulation is one of the few characteristics that we share with dogs, and I think of Anson on that day as some well-bred specimen who had been disappointed at a familiar back door. He was going to see Nick, once a fashionable bartender in demand at all private dances, and now employed in cooling non-alcoholic champagne among the labyrinthine cellars of the Plaza Hotel.

'Nick,' he said, 'what's happened to everything?'

'Dead,' Nick said.

'Make me a whiskey sour.' Anson handed a pint bottle over the counter. 'Nick, the girls are different; I had a little girl in Brooklyn and she got married last week without letting me know.'

'That a fact? Ha-ha-ha,' responded Nick diplomatically. 'Slipped it over on you.'

'Absolutely,' said Anson. 'And I was out with her the night before.'

'Ha-ha-ha,' said Nick, 'ha-ha-ha!'

'Do you remember the wedding, Nick, in Hot Springs

where I had the waiters and the musicians singing *God Save the King*?'

'Now where was that, Mr Hunter?' Nick concentrated doubtfully. 'Seems to me that was –'

'Next time they were back for more, and I began to wonder how much I'd paid them,' continued Anson.

'– seems to me that was at Mr Trenholm's wedding.'

'Don't know him,' said Anson decisively. He was offended that a strange name should intrude upon his reminiscences; Nick perceived this.

'Na – aw –' he admitted, 'I ought to know that. It was one of *your* crowd – Brakins… Baker –'

'Bicker Baker,' said Anson responsively. 'They put me in a hearse after it was over and covered me up with flowers and drove me away.'

'Ha-ha-ha,' said Nick. 'Ha-ha-ha.'

Nick's simulation of the old family servant paled presently and Anson went upstairs to the lobby. He looked around – his eyes met the glance of an unfamiliar clerk at the desk, then fell upon a flower from the morning's marriage hesitating in the mouth of a brass cuspidor. He went out and walked slowly towards the blood-red sun over Columbus Circle. Suddenly he turned around and, retracing his steps to the Plaza, immured himself in a telephone booth.

Later he said that he tried to get me three times that afternoon, that he tried everyone who might be in New York – men and girls he had not seen for years, an artist's model of his college days whose faded number was still in his address book – Central told him that even the exchange existed no longer. At length his quest roved into the country, and he held brief disappointing conversations with emphatic butlers and maids. So-and-so was out, riding, swimming, playing golf, sailed to Europe last week. Who shall I say phoned?'

It was intolerable that he should pass the evening alone –
the private reckonings which one plans for a moment of leisure
lose every charm when the solitude is enforced. There were
always women of a sort, but the ones he knew had temporarily
vanished, and to pass a New York evening in the hired company of a stranger never occurred to him – he would have
considered that that was something shameful and secret, the
diversion of a travelling salesman in a strange town.

Anson paid the telephone bill – the girl tried unsuccessfully
to joke with him about its size – and for the second time that
afternoon started to leave the Plaza and go he knew not where.
Near the revolving door the figure of a woman, obviously with
child, stood sideways to the light – a sheer beige cape fluttered
at her shoulders when the door turned and, each time, she
looked impatiently towards it as if she were weary of waiting.
At the first sight of her a strong nervous thrill of familiarity
went over him, but not until he was within five feet of her did
he realise that it was Paula.

'Why, Anson Hunter!'

His heart turned over.

'Why, Paula –'

'Why, this is wonderful. I can't believe it, *Anson*!'

She took both his hands, and he saw in the freedom of
the gesture that the memory of him had lost poignancy to her.
But not to him – he felt that old mood that she evoked in him
stealing over his brain, that gentleness with which he had
always met her optimism as if afraid to mar its surface.

'We're at Rye for the summer. Pete had to come East on
business – you know of course I'm Mrs Peter Hagerty now –
so we brought the children and took a house. You've got to
come out and see us.'

'Can I?' he asked directly. 'When?'

'When you like. Here's Pete.' The revolving door functioned, giving up a fine tall man of thirty with a tanned face and a trim moustache. His immaculate fitness made a sharp contrast with Anson's increasing bulk, which was obvious under the faintly tight cut-away coat.

'You oughtn't to be standing,' said Hagerty to his wife. 'Let's sit down here.' He indicated lobby chairs, but Paula hesitated.

'I've got to go right home,' she said. 'Anson, why don't you – why don't you come out and have dinner with us tonight! We're just getting settled, but if you can stand that –'

Hagerty confirmed the invitation cordially.

'Come out for the night.'

Their car waited in front of the hotel, and Paula with a tired gesture sank back against silk cushions in the corner. 'There's so much I want to talk to you about,' she said, 'it seems hopeless.'

'I want to hear about you.'

'Well' – she smiled at Hagerty – 'that would take a long time too. I have three children – by my first marriage. The oldest is five, then four, then three.' She smiled again. 'I didn't waste much time having them, did I?'

'Boys?'

'A boy and two girls. Then – oh, a lot of things happened, and I got a divorce in Paris a year ago and married Pete. That's all – except that I'm awfully happy.'

In Rye they drove up to a large house near the Beach Club, from which there issued presently three dark, slim children who broke from an English governess and approached them with an esoteric cry. Abstractedly and with difficulty, Paula took each one into her arms, a caress which they accepted stiffly, as they had evidently been told not to bump into

Mummy. Even against their fresh faces Paula's skin showed scarcely any weariness – for all her physical languor she seemed younger than when he had last seen her at Palm Beach seven years ago.

At dinner she was preoccupied, and afterwards, during the homage to the radio, she lay with closed eyes on the sofa, until Anson wondered if his presence at this time were not an intrusion. But at nine o'clock, when Hagerty rose and said pleasantly that he was going to leave them by themselves for a while, she began to talk slowly about herself and the past.

'My first baby,' she said – 'the one we call Darling, the biggest little girl – I wanted to die when I knew I was going to have her, because Lowell was like a stranger to me. It didn't seem as though she could be my own. I wrote you a letter and tore it up. Oh, you were *so* bad to me, Anson.'

It was the dialogue again, rising and falling, Anson felt a sudden quickening of memory.

'Weren't you engaged once?' she asked – 'a girl named Dolly something?'

'I wasn't ever engaged. I tried to be engaged, but I never loved anybody but you, Paula.'

'Oh,' she said. Then after a moment: 'This baby is the first one I ever really wanted. You see, I'm in love now – at last.'

He didn't answer, shocked at the treachery of her remembrance. She must have seen that the 'at last' bruised him, for she continued:

'I was infatuated with you, Anson – you could make me do anything you liked. But we wouldn't have been happy. I'm not smart enough for you. I don't like things to be complicated like you do.' She paused. 'You'll never settle down,' she said.

The phrase struck at him from behind – it was an accusation that of all accusations he had never merited.

45

'I could settle down if women were different,' he said. 'If I didn't understand so much about them, if women didn't spoil you for other women, if they had only a little pride. If I could go to sleep for a while and wake up into a home that was really mine – why, that's what I'm made for, Paula, that's what women have seen in me and liked in me. It's only that I can't get through the preliminaries any more.'

Hagerty came in a little before eleven; after a whiskey Paula stood up and announced that she was going to bed. She went over and stood by her husband.

'Where did you go, dearest?' she demanded.

'I had a drink with Ed Saunders.'

'I was worried. I thought maybe you'd run away.'

She rested her head against his coat.

'He's sweet, isn't he, Anson?' she demanded.

'Absolutely,' said Anson, laughing.

She raised her face to her husband.

'Well, I'm ready,' she said. She turned to Anson: 'Do you want to see our family gymnastic stunt?'

'Yes,' he said in an interested voice.

'All right. Here we go!'

Hagerty picked her up easily in his arms.

'This is called the family acrobatic stunt,' said Paula. 'He carries me upstairs. Isn't it sweet of him?'

'Yes,' said Anson.

Hagerty bent his head slightly until his face touched Paula's.

'And I love him,' she said. 'I've just been telling you haven't I, Anson?'

'Yes,' he said.

'He's the dearest thing that ever lived in this world; aren't you, darling?... Well, goodnight. Here we go. Isn't he strong?'

'Yes,' Anson said.

'You'll find a pair of Pete's pyjamas laid out for you. Sweet dreams – see you at breakfast.'

'Yes,' Anson said.

### 8

The older members of the firm insisted that Anson should go abroad for the summer. He had scarcely had a vacation in seven years, they said. He was stale and needed a change. Anson resisted.

'If I go,' he declared, 'I won't come back any more.'

'That's absurd, old man. You'll be back in three months with all this depression gone. Fit as ever.'

'No.' He shook his head stubbornly. 'If I stop, I won't go back to work. If I stop, that means I've given up – I'm through.'

'We'll take a chance on that. Stay six months if you like – we're not afraid you'll leave us. Why, you'd be miserable if you didn't work.'

They arranged his passage for him. They liked Anson – everyone liked Anson – and the change that had been coming over him cast a sort of pall over the office. The enthusiasm that had invariably signalled up business, the consideration towards his equals and his inferiors, the lift of his vital presence – within the past four months his intense nervousness had melted down these qualities into the fussy pessimism of a man of forty. On every transaction in which he was involved he acted as a drag and a strain.

'If I go I'll never come back,' he said.

Three days before he sailed Paula Legendre Hagerty died in childbirth. I was with him a great deal then, for we were crossing together, but for the first time in our friendship he told me not a word of how he felt, nor did I see the slightest sign of emotion. His chief preoccupation was with the fact that he was thirty years old – he would turn the conversation to the point where he could remind you of it and then fall silent, as if he assumed that the statement would start a chain of thought sufficient to itself. Like his partners, I was amazed at the change in him, and I was glad when the *Paris* moved off into the wet space between the worlds, leaving his principality behind.

'How about a drink?' he suggested.

We walked into the bar with that defiant feeling that characterises the day of departure and ordered four Martinis. After one cocktail a change came over him – he suddenly reached across and slapped my knee with the first joviality I had seen him exhibit for months.

'Did you see the girl in the red tam?' he demanded, 'the one with the high colour who had the two police dogs down to bid her goodbye.'

'She's pretty,' I agreed.

'I looked her up in the purser's office and found out that she's alone. I'm going down to see the steward in a few minutes. We'll have dinner with her tonight.'

After a while he left me, and within an hour he was walking up and down the deck with her, talking to her in his strong, clear voice. Her red tam was a bright spot of colour against the steel-grey sea, and from time to time she looked up with a flashing bob of her head, and smiled with amusement and interest, and anticipation. At dinner we had champagne, and were very joyous – afterwards Anson ran the pool with infectious gusto, and several people who had seen me with him asked me his name. He and the girl were talking and laughing together on a lounge in the bar when I went to bed.

I saw less of him on the trip than I had hoped. He wanted to arrange a foursome, but there was no one available, so I saw him only at meals. Sometimes, though, he would have a cocktail in the bar, and he told me about the girl in the red tam, and his adventures with her, making them all bizarre and amusing, as he had a way of doing, and I was glad that he was himself again, or at least the self that I knew, and with which I felt at home. I don't think he was ever happy unless someone was in love with him, responding to him like filings to a magnet, helping him to explain himself, promising him something. What it was I do not know. Perhaps they promised that there would always be women in the world who would spend their brightest, freshest, rarest, hours to nurse and protect that superiority he cherished in his heart.

# The Bridal Party

There was the usual insincere little note saying: 'I wanted you to be the first to know.' It was a double shock to Michael, announcing, as it did, both the engagement and the imminent marriage; which, moreover, was to be held, not in New York, decently and far away, but here in Paris under his very nose, if that could be said to extend over the Protestant Episcopal Church of the Holy Trinity, avenue George V. The date was two weeks off, early in June.

At first Michael was afraid and his stomach felt hollow. When he left the hotel that morning, the *femme de chambre*, who was in love with his fine, sharp profile and his pleasant buoyancy, scented the hard abstraction that had settled over him. He walked in a daze to his bank, he bought a detective story at Smith's on the rue de Rivoli, he sympathetically stared for a while at a faded panorama of the battlefields in a tourist-office window and cursed a Greek tout who followed him with a half-displayed packet of innocuous postcards warranted to be very dirty indeed.

But the fear stayed with him, and after a while he recognised it as the fear that now he would never be happy. He had met Caroline Dandy when she was seventeen, possessed her young heart all through her first season in New York, and then lost her, slowly, tragically, uselessly, because he had no money and could make no money; because, with all the energy and goodwill in the world, he could not find himself; because, loving him still, Caroline had lost faith and begun to see him as something pathetic, futile and shabby, outside the great, shining stream of life towards which she was inevitably drawn.

Since his only support was that she loved him, he leant weakly on that; the support broke, but still he held onto it and was carried out to sea and washed up on the French coast with its broken pieces still in his hands. He carried them around with him in the form of photographs and packets of correspondence and a liking for a maudlin popular song called 'Among My Souvenirs'. He kept clear of other girls, as if Caroline would somehow know it and reciprocate with a faithful heart. Her note informed him that he had lost her for ever.

It was a fine morning. In front of the shops in the rue de Castiglione, proprietors and patrons were on the sidewalk gazing upward, for the Graf Zeppelin, shining and glorious, symbol of escape and destruction – of escape, if necessary, through destruction – glided in the Paris sky. He heard a woman say in French that it would not her astonish if that commenced to let fall the bombs. Then he heard another voice, full of husky laughter, and the void in his stomach froze. Jerking about, he was face to face with Caroline Dandy and her fiancé.

'Why, Michael! Why, we were wondering where you were. I asked at the Guaranty Trust, and Morgan and Company, and finally sent a note to the National City –'

Why didn't they back away? Why didn't they back right up, walking backwards down the rue de Castiglione, across the rue de Rivoli, through the Tuileries Gardens, still walking backwards as fast as they could till they grew vague and faded out across the river?

'This is Hamilton Rutherford, my fiancé.'

'We've met before.'

'At Pat's, wasn't it?'

'And last spring in the Ritz Bar.'

'Michael, where have you been keeping yourself?'

'Around here.' This agony. Previews of Hamilton

Rutherford flashed before his eyes – a quick series of pictures, sentences. He remembered hearing that he had bought a seat in 1920 for a hundred and twenty-five thousand of borrowed money, and just before the break sold it for more than half a million. Not handsome like Michael, but vitally attractive, confident, authoritative, just the right height over Caroline there – Michael had always been too short for Caroline when they danced.

Rutherford was saying: 'No, I'd like it very much if you'd come to the bachelor dinner. I'm taking the Ritz Bar from nine o'clock on. Then right after the wedding there'll be a reception and breakfast at the Hotel George V.'

'And, Michael, George Packman is giving a party day after tomorrow at Chez Victor, and I want you to be sure and come. And also to tea Friday at Jebby West's; she'd want to have you if she knew where you were. What's your hotel, so we can send you an invitation? You see, the reason we decided to have it over here is because Mother has been sick in a nursing home here and the whole clan is in Paris. Then Hamilton's mother's being here too –'

The entire clan; they had always hated him, except her mother; always discouraged his courtship. What a little counter he was in this game of families and money! Under his hat his brow sweated with the humiliation of the fact that for all his misery he was worth just exactly so many invitations. Frantically he began to mumble something about going away.

Then it happened – Caroline saw deep into him, and Michael knew that she saw. She saw through to his profound woundedness, and something quivered inside her, died out along the curve of her mouth and in her eyes. He had moved her. All the unforgettable impulses of first love had surged up once more; their hearts had in some way touched across two feet of Paris sunlight. She took her fiancé's arm suddenly, as if to steady herself with the feel of it.

They parted. Michael walked quickly for a minute; then he stopped, pretending to look in a window, and saw them further up the street, walking fast into the Place Vendôme, people with much to do.

He had things to do also – he had to get his laundry.

'Nothing will ever be the same again,' he said to himself. 'She will never be happy in her marriage and I will never be happy at all any more.'

The two vivid years of his love for Caroline moved back around him like years in Einstein's physics. Intolerable memories arose – of rides in the Long Island moonlight; of a happy time at Lake Placid with her cheeks so cold there, but warm just underneath the surface; of a despairing afternoon in a little café on 48th Street in the last sad months when their marriage had come to seem impossible.

'Come in,' he said aloud.

The concierge with a telegram; brusque because Mr Curly's clothes were a little shabby. Mr Curly gave few tips; Mr Curly was obviously a *petit client*.

Michael read the telegram.

'An answer?' the concierge asked.

'No,' said Michael, and then, on an impulse: 'Look.'

'Too bad – too bad,' said the concierge. 'Your grandfather is dead.'

'Not too bad,' said Michael. 'It means that I come into a quarter of a million dollars.'

Too late by a single month; after the first flush of the news his misery was deeper than ever. Lying awake in bed that night, he listened endlessly to the long caravan of a circus moving through the street from one Paris fair to another.

When the last van had rumbled out of hearing and the corners of the furniture were pastel blue with the dawn, he was still thinking of the look in Caroline's eyes that morning – the look that seemed to say: 'Oh, why couldn't you have done something about it? Why couldn't you have been stronger, made me marry you? Don't you see how sad I am?'

Michael's fists clenched.

'Well, I won't give up till the last moment,' he whispered. 'I've had all the bad luck so far, and maybe it's turned at last. One takes what one can get, up to the limit of one's strength, and if I can't have her, at least she'll go into marriage with some of me in her heart.'

2

Accordingly he went to the party at Chez Victor two days later, upstairs and into the little salon off the bar where the party was to assemble for cocktails. He was early; the only other occupant was a tall lean man of fifty. They spoke.

'You waiting for George Packman's party?'

'Yes. My name's Michael Curly.'

'My name's –'

Michael failed to catch the name. They ordered a drink, and Michael supposed that the bride and groom were having a gay time.

'Too much so,' the other agreed, frowning. 'I don't see how they stand it. We all crossed on the boat together; five days of that crazy life and then two weeks of Paris. You' – he hesitated, smiling faintly – 'you'll excuse me for saying that your generation drinks too much.'

'Not Caroline.'

'No, not Caroline. She seems to take only a cocktail and a glass of champagne, and then she's had enough, thank God. But Hamilton drinks too much and all this crowd of young people drink too much. Do you live in Paris?'

'For the moment,' said Michael.

'I don't like Paris. My wife – that is to say, my ex-wife, Hamilton's mother – lives in Paris.'

'You're Hamilton Rutherford's father?'

'I have that honour. And I'm not denying that I'm proud of what he's done; it was just a general comment.'

'Of course.'

Michael glanced up nervously as four people came in. He felt suddenly that his dinner coat was old and shiny; he had ordered a new one that morning. The people who had come in were rich and at home in their richness with one another – a dark, lovely girl with a hysterical little laugh whom he had met before; two confident men whose jokes referred invariably to last night's scandal and tonight's potentialities, as if they had important roles in a play that extended indefinitely into the past and the future. When Caroline arrived, Michael had scarcely a moment of her, but it was enough to note that, like all the others, she was strained and tired. She was pale beneath her rouge; there were shadows under her eyes. With a mixture of relief and wounded vanity, he found himself placed far from her and at another table; he needed a moment to adjust himself to his surroundings. This was not like the immature set in which he and Caroline had moved; the men were more than thirty and had an air of sharing the best of this world's good. Next to him was Jebby West, whom he knew; and, on the other side, a jovial man who immediately began to talk to Michael about a stunt for the bachelor dinner: they were going to hire a French girl to appear with an actual baby in her arms,

58

crying: 'Hamilton, you can't desert me now!' The idea seemed stale and unamusing to Michael, but its originator shook with anticipatory laughter.

Further up the table there was talk of the market – another drop today, the most appreciable since the crash; people were kidding Rutherford about it: 'Too bad, old man. You better not get married, after all.'

Michael asked the man on his left, 'Has he lost a lot?'

'Nobody knows. He's heavily involved, but he's one of the smartest young men in Wall Street. Anyhow, nobody ever tells you the truth.'

It was a champagne dinner from the start, and towards the end it reached a pleasant level of conviviality, but Michael saw that all these people were too weary to be exhilarated by any ordinary stimulant; for weeks they had drunk cocktails before meals like Americans, wines and brandies like Frenchmen, beer like Germans, whiskey-and-soda like the English, and as they were no longer in the twenties, this preposterous *mélange*, that was like some gigantic cocktail in a nightmare, served only to make them temporarily less conscious of the mistakes of the night before. Which is to say that it was not really a gay party; what gaiety existed was displayed in the few who drank nothing at all.

But Michael was not tired, and the champagne stimulated him and made his misery less acute. He had been away from New York for more than eight months and most of the dance music was unfamiliar to him, but at the first bars of the 'Painted Doll', to which he and Caroline had moved through so much happiness and despair the previous summer, he crossed to Caroline's table and asked her to dance.

She was lovely in a dress of thin ethereal blue, and the proximity of her crackly yellow hair, of her cool and tender grey eyes, turned his body clumsy and rigid; he stumbled with their first step on the floor. For a moment it seemed that there was nothing to say; he wanted to tell her about his inheritance, but the idea seemed abrupt, unprepared for.

'Michael, it's so nice to be dancing with you again.'

He smiled grimly.

'I'm so happy you came,' she continued. 'I was afraid maybe you'd be silly and stay away. Now we can be just good friends and natural together. Michael, I want you and Hamilton to like each other.'

The engagement was making her stupid; he had never heard her make such a series of obvious remarks before.

'I could kill him without a qualm,' he said pleasantly, 'but he looks like a good man. He's fine. What I want to know is, what happens to people like me who aren't able to forget?'

As he said this he could not prevent his mouth from drooping suddenly, and glancing up, Caroline saw, and her heart quivered violently, as it had the other morning.

'Do you mind so much, Michael?'

'Yes.'

For a second as he said this, in a voice that seemed to have come up from his shoes, they were not dancing; they were simply clinging together. Then she leant away from him and twisted her mouth into a lovely smile.

'I didn't know what to do at first, Michael. I told Hamilton about you – that I'd cared for you an awful lot – but it didn't worry him, and he was right. Because I'm over you now – yes, I am. And you'll wake up some sunny morning and be over me just like that.'

He shook his head stubbornly.

'Oh, yes. We weren't for each other. I'm pretty flighty, and I need somebody like Hamilton to decide things. It was that more than the question of – of –'

'Of money.' Again he was on the point of telling her what had happened, but again something told him that it was not the time.

'Then how do you account for what happened when we met the other day,' he demanded helplessly – 'what happened just now? When we just pour towards each other like we used to – as if we were one person, as if the same blood was flowing through both of us?'

'Oh, don't,' she begged him. 'You mustn't talk like that; everything's decided now. I love Hamilton with all my heart. It's just that I remember certain things in the past and I feel sorry for you – for us – for the way we were.'

Over her shoulder, Michael saw a man come towards them to cut in. In a panic he danced her away, but inevitably the man came on.

'I've got to see you alone, if only for a minute,' Michael said quickly. 'When can I?'

'I'll be at Jebby West's tea tomorrow,' she whispered as a hand fell politely upon Michael's shoulder.

But he did not talk to her at Jebby West's tea. Rutherford stood next to her, and each brought the other into all conversations. They left early. The next morning the wedding cards arrived in the first mail.

Then Michael, grown desperate with pacing up and down his room, determined on a bold stroke; he wrote to Hamilton Rutherford, asking him for a rendezvous the following afternoon. In a short telephone communication Rutherford agreed, but for a day later than Michael had asked. And the wedding was only six days away.

They were to meet in the bar of the Hotel Jena. Michael knew what he would say: 'See here, Rutherford, do you realise the responsibility you're taking in going through with this marriage? Do you realise the harvest of trouble and regret you're sowing in persuading a girl into something contrary to the instincts of her heart?' He would explain that the barrier between Caroline and himself had been an artificial one and was now removed, and demand that the matter be put up to Caroline frankly before it was too late.

Rutherford would be angry, conceivably there would be a scene, but Michael felt that he was fighting for life now.

He found Rutherford in conversation with an older man, whom Michael had met at several of the wedding parties.

'I saw what happened to most of my friends,' Rutherford was saying, 'and I decided it wasn't going to happen to me. It isn't so difficult; if you take a girl with common sense, and tell her what's what, and do your stuff damn well, and play decently square with her, it's a marriage. If you stand for any nonsense at the beginning, it's one of these arrangements – within five years the man gets out, or else the girl gobbles him up and you have the usual mess.'

'Right!' agreed his companion enthusiastically. 'Hamilton, boy, you're right.'

Michael's blood boiled slowly.

'Doesn't it strike you,' he enquired coldly, 'that your attitude went out of fashion about a hundred years ago?'

'No, it didn't,' said Rutherford pleasantly, but impatiently. 'I'm as modern as anybody. I'd get married in an aeroplane next Saturday if it'd please my girl.'

'I don't mean that way of being modern. You can't take a sensitive woman –'

'Sensitive? Women aren't so darn sensitive. It's fellows like you who are sensitive; it's fellows like you they exploit – all your devotion and kindness and all that. They read a couple of books and see a few pictures because they haven't got anything else to do, and then they say they're finer in grain than you are, and to prove it they take the bit in their teeth and tear off for a fare-you-well – just about as sensitive as a fire horse.'

'Caroline happens to be sensitive,' said Michael in a clipped voice.

At this point the other man got up to go; when the dispute about the check had been settled and they were alone, Rutherford leant back to Michael as if a question had been asked him.

'Caroline's more than sensitive,' he said. 'She's got sense.'

His combative eyes, meeting Michael's, flickered with a grey light. 'This all sounds pretty crude to you, Mr Curly, but it seems to me that the average man nowadays just asks to be made a monkey of by some woman who doesn't even get any fun out of reducing him to that level. There are darn few men who possess their wives any more, but I'm going to be one of them.'

To Michael it seemed time to bring the talk back to the actual situation: 'Do you realise the responsibility you're taking?'

'I certainly do,' interrupted Rutherford. 'I'm not afraid of responsibility. I'll make the decisions – fairly, I hope, but anyhow they'll be final.'

'What if you didn't start right?' said Michael impetuously. 'What if your marriage isn't founded on mutual love?'

'I think I see what you mean,' Rutherford said, still pleasant. 'And since you've brought it up, let me say that if you and Caroline had married, it wouldn't have lasted three years. Do you know what your affair was founded on? On sorrow. You got sorry for each other. Sorrow's a lot of fun for most women and for some men, but it seems to me that a marriage ought to be based on hope.' He looked at his watch and stood up.

'I've got to meet Caroline. Remember, you're coming to the bachelor dinner day after tomorrow.'

Michael felt the moment slipping away. 'Then Caroline's personal feelings don't count with you?' he demanded fiercely.

'Caroline's tired and upset. But she has what she wants, and that's the main thing.'

'Are you referring to yourself?' demanded Michael incredulously.

'Yes.'

'May I ask how long she's wanted you?'

'About two years.' Before Michael could answer, he was gone.

During the next two days Michael floated in an abyss of helplessness. The idea haunted him that he had left something undone that would sever this knot drawn tighter under his eyes. He phoned Caroline, but she insisted that it was physically impossible for her to see him until the day before the wedding, for which day she granted him a tentative rendezvous. Then he went to the bachelor dinner, partly in fear of an evening alone at his hotel, partly from a feeling that by his presence at that function he was somehow nearer to Caroline, keeping her in sight.

The Ritz Bar had been prepared for the occasion by French and American banners and by a great canvas covering one wall, against which the guests were invited to concentrate their proclivities in breaking glasses.

At the first cocktail, taken at the bar, there were many slight spillings from many hands, but later, with the champagne, there was a rising tide of laughter and occasional bursts of song.

Michael was surprised to find what a difference his new dinner coat, his new silk hat, his new, proud linen made in his estimate of himself; he felt less resentment towards all these people for being so rich and assured. For the first time since he had left college he felt rich and assured himself; he felt that he was part of all this, and even entered into the scheme of Johnson, the practical joker, for the appearance of the woman betrayed, now waiting tranquilly in the room across the hall.

'We don't want to go too heavy,' Johnson said, 'because I imagine Ham's had a pretty anxious day already. Did you see Fullman Oil's sixteen points off this morning?'

'Will that matter to him?' Michael asked, trying to keep the interest out of his voice.

'Naturally. He's in heavily; he's always in everything heavily. So far he's had luck; anyhow, up to a month ago.'

The glasses were filled and emptied faster now, and men were shouting at one another across the narrow table. Against the bar a group of ushers was being photographed, and the flashlight surged through the room in a stifling cloud.

'Now's the time,' Johnson said. 'You're to stand by the door, remember, and we're both to try and keep her from coming in – just till we get everyone's attention.'

He went out into the corridor, and Michael waited obediently by the door. Several minutes passed. Then Johnson reappeared with a curious expression on his face.

'There's something funny about this.'

'Isn't the girl there?'

'She's there all right, but there's another woman there, too; and it's nobody we engaged either. She wants to see Hamilton Rutherford, and she looks as if she had something on her mind.'

They went out into the hall. Planted firmly in a chair near

the door sat an American girl a little the worse for liquor, but with a determined expression on her face. She looked up at them with a jerk of her head.

'Well, j'tell him?' she demanded. 'The name is Marjorie Collins, and he'll know it. I've come a long way, and I want to see him now and quick, or there's going to be more trouble than you ever saw.' She rose unsteadily to her feet.

'You go in and tell Ham,' whispered Johnson to Michael. 'Maybe he'd better get out. I'll keep her here.'

Back at the table, Michael leant close to Rutherford's ear and, with a certain grimness, whispered:

'A girl outside named Marjorie Collins says she wants to see you. She looks as if she wanted to make trouble.'

Hamilton Rutherford blinked and his mouth fell ajar; then slowly the lips came together in a straight line and he said in a crisp voice:

'Please keep her there. And send the head barman to me right away.'

Michael spoke to the barman, and then, without returning to the table, asked quietly for his coat and hat. Out in the hall again, he passed Johnson and the girl without speaking and went out into the rue Cambon. Calling a cab, he gave the address of Caroline's hotel.

His place was beside her now. Not to bring bad news, but simply to be with her when her house of cards came falling around her head.

Rutherford had implied that he was soft – well, he was hard enough not to give up the girl he loved without taking advantage of every chance within the pale of honour. Should she turn away from Rutherford, she would find him there.

She was in; she was surprised when he called, but she was still dressed and would be down immediately. Presently she appeared in a dinner gown, holding two blue telegrams in her hand. They sat down in armchairs in the deserted lobby.

'But, Michael, is the dinner over?'

'I wanted to see you, so I came away.'

'I'm glad.' Her voice was friendly, but matter-of-fact. 'Because I'd just phoned your hotel that I had fittings and rehearsals all day tomorrow. Now we can have our talk after all.'

'You're tired,' he guessed. 'Perhaps I shouldn't have come.'

'No. I was waiting up for Hamilton. Telegrams that may be important. He said he might go on somewhere, and that may mean any hour, so I'm glad I have someone to talk to.'

Michael winced at the impersonality in that last phrase.

'Don't you care when he gets home?'

'Naturally,' she said, laughing, 'but I haven't got much say about it, have I?'

'Why not?'

'I couldn't start by telling him what he could and couldn't do.'

'Why not?'

'He wouldn't stand for it.'

'He seems to want merely a housekeeper,' said Michael ironically.

'Tell me about your plans, Michael,' she asked quickly.

'My plans? I can't see any future after the day after to-morrow. The only real plan I ever had was to love you.'

Their eyes brushed past each other's, and the look he knew so well was staring out at him from hers. Words flowed quickly from his heart:

'Let me tell you just once more how well I've loved you, never wavering for a moment, never thinking of another girl. And now when I think of all the years ahead without you, without any hope, I don't want to live, Caroline darling. I used to dream about our home, our children, about holding you in my arms and touching your face and hands and hair that used to belong to me, and now I just can't wake up.'

Caroline was crying softly. 'Poor Michael – poor Michael.' Her hand reached out and her fingers brushed the lapel of his dinner coat. 'I was so sorry for you the other night. You looked so thin, and as if you needed a new suit and somebody to take care of you.' She sniffled and looked more closely at his coat. 'Why, you've got a new suit! And a new silk hat! Why, Michael, how swell!' She laughed, suddenly cheerful through her tears. 'You must have come into money, Michael; I never saw you so well turned out.'

For a moment, at her reaction, he hated his new clothes.

'I have come into money,' he said. 'My grandfather left me about a quarter of a million dollars.'

'Why, Michael,' she cried, 'how perfectly swell! I can't tell you how glad I am. I've always thought you were the sort of person who ought to have money.'

'Yes, just too late to make a difference.'

The revolving door from the street groaned around and Hamilton Rutherford came into the lobby. His face was flushed, his eyes were restless and impatient.

'Hello, darling; hello, Mr Curly.' He bent and kissed Caroline. 'I broke away for a minute to find out if I had any telegrams. I see you've got them there.' Taking them from her, he remarked to Curly, 'That was an odd business in the bar, wasn't it? Especially as I understand some of you had a joke fixed up in the same line.' He opened one of the telegrams, closed it and turned to Caroline with the divided expression of a man carrying two things in his head at once.

'A girl I haven't seen for two years turned up,' he said. 'It seemed to be some clumsy form of blackmail, for I haven't and never have had any sort of obligation toward her whatever.'

'What happened?'

'The head barman had a Sûreté Générale man there in ten minutes and it was settled in the hall. The French blackmail laws make ours look like a sweet wish, and I gather they threw a scare into her that she'll remember. But it seems wiser to tell you.'

'Are you implying that I mentioned the matter?' said Michael stiffly.

'No,' Rutherford said slowly. 'No, you were just going to be on hand. And since you're here, I'll tell you some news that will interest you even more.'

He handed Michael one telegram and opened the other.

'This is in code,' Michael said.

'So is this. But I've got to know all the words pretty well this last week. The two of them together mean that I'm due to start life all over.'

Michael saw Caroline's face grow a shade paler, but she sat quiet as a mouse.

'It was a mistake and I stuck to it too long,' continued Rutherford. 'So you see I don't have all the luck, Mr Curly. By the way, they tell me you've come into money.'

'Yes,' said Michael.

'There we are, then.' Rutherford turned to Caroline. 'You understand, darling, that I'm not joking or exaggerating. I've lost almost every cent I had and I'm starting life over.'

Two pairs of eyes were regarding her – Rutherford's non-committal and unrequiring, Michael's hungry, tragic, pleading. In a minute she had raised herself from the chair and with a little cry thrown herself into Hamilton Rutherford's arms.

'Oh, darling,' she cried, 'what does it matter! It's better; I like it better, honestly I do! I want to start that way; I want to! Oh, please don't worry or be sad even for a minute!'

'All right, baby,' said Rutherford. His hand stroked her hair gently for a moment; then he took his arm from around her.

'I promised to join the party for an hour,' he said. 'So I'll say goodnight, and I want you to go to bed soon and get a good sleep. Goodnight, Mr Curly. I'm sorry to have let you in for all these financial matters.'

But Michael had already picked up his hat and cane. 'I'll go along with you,' he said.


### 3


It was such a fine morning. Michael's cut-away hadn't been delivered, so he felt rather uncomfortable passing before the cameras and moving-picture machines in front of the little church on the avenue George V.

It was such a clean, new church that it seemed unforgivable not to be dressed properly, and Michael, white and shaky after a sleepless night, decided to stand in the rear. From there he looked at the back of Hamilton Rutherford, and the lacy, filmy back of Caroline, and the fat back of George Packman, which looked unsteady, as if it wanted to lean against the bride and groom.

The ceremony went on for a long time under the gay flags and pennons overhead, under the thick beams of June sunlight slanting down through the tall windows upon the well-dressed people.

As the procession, headed by the bride and groom, started down the aisle, Michael realised with alarm he was just where everyone would dispense with their parade stiffness, become informal and speak to him.

So it turned out. Rutherford and Caroline spoke first to him; Rutherford grim with the strain of being married, and Caroline lovelier than he had ever seen her, floating all softly down through the friends and relatives of her youth, down through the past and forward to the future by the sunlit door.

Michael managed to murmur, 'Beautiful, simply beautiful,' and then other people passed and spoke to him – old Mrs Dandy, straight from her sickbed and looking remarkably well, or carrying it off like the very fine old lady she was; and Rutherford's father and mother, ten years divorced, but walking side by side and looking made for each other and proud. Then all Caroline's sisters and their husbands and her little nephews in Eton suits, and then a long parade, all speaking to Michael because he was still standing paralysed just at that point where the procession broke.

He wondered what would happen now. Cards had been issued for a reception at the George V; an expensive enough place, Heaven knew. Would Rutherford try to go through with that on top of those disastrous telegrams? Evidently, for the procession outside was streaming up there through the June morning, three by three and four by four. On the corner the long dresses of girls, five abreast, fluttered many-coloured in the wind. Girls had become gossamer again, perambulatory flora; such lovely fluttering dresses in the bright noon wind.

Michael needed a drink; he couldn't face that reception line without a drink. Diving into a side doorway of the hotel, he asked for the bar, whither a chasseur led him through half a kilometre of new American-looking passages.

But – how did it happen? – the bar was full. There were ten – fifteen men and two – four girls, all from the wedding, all needing a drink. There were cocktails and champagne in the bar; Rutherford's cocktails and champagne, as it turned out, for he had engaged the whole bar and the ballroom and the two great reception rooms and all the stairways leading up and down, and windows looking out over the whole square block of Paris. By and by Michael went and joined the long, slow drift of the receiving line. Through a flowery mist of 'Such a lovely wedding', 'My dear, you were simply lovely', 'You're a lucky man, Rutherford', he passed down the line. When Michael came to Caroline, she took a single step forward and kissed him on the lips, but he felt no contact in the kiss; it was unreal and he floated on away from it. Old Mrs Dandy, who had always liked him, held his hand for a minute and thanked him for the flowers he had sent when he heard she was ill.

'I'm so sorry not to have written; you know, we old ladies are grateful for –' The flowers, the fact that she had not written, the wedding – Michael saw that they all had the same relative importance to her now; she had married off five other children and seen two of the marriages go to pieces, and this scene, so poignant, so confusing to Michael, appeared to her simply a familiar charade in which she had played her part before.

A buffet luncheon with champagne was already being served at small tables and there was an orchestra playing in the empty ballroom. Michael sat down with Jebby West; he was still a little embarrassed at not wearing a morning coat, but he perceived now that he was not alone in the omission and felt better. 'Wasn't Caroline divine?' Jebby West said. 'So entirely self-possessed. I asked her this morning if she wasn't a little nervous at stepping off like this. And she said, "Why should I be? I've been after him for two years, and now I'm just happy that's all." '

'It must be true,' said Michael gloomily.

'What?'

'What you just said.'

He had been stabbed, but, rather to his distress, he did not feel the wound.

He asked Jebby to dance. Out on the floor, Rutherford's father and mother were dancing together.

'It makes me a little sad, that,' she said. 'Those two hadn't met for years; both of them were married again and she divorced again. She went to the station to meet him when he came over for Caroline's wedding, and invited him to stay at her house in the avenue du Bois with a whole lot of other people, perfectly proper, but he was afraid his wife would hear about it and not like it, so he went to a hotel. Don't you think that's sort of sad?'

An hour or so later Michael realised suddenly that it was afternoon. In one corner of the ballroom an arrangement of screens like a moving-picture stage had been set up and photographers were taking official pictures of the bridal party. The bridal party, still as death and pale as wax under the bright lights, appeared, to the dancers circling the modulated semi-darkness of the ballroom, like those jovial or sinister groups that one comes upon in The Old Mill at an amusement park.

After the bridal party had been photographed, there was a group of the ushers; then the bridesmaids, the families, the children. Later, Caroline, active and excited, having long since abandoned the repose implicit in her flowing dress and great bouquet, came and plucked Michael off the floor.

'Now we'll have them take one of just old friends.' Her voice implied that this was best, most intimate of all. 'Come here, Jebby, George – not you, Hamilton; this is just my friends – Sally –'

73

A little after that, what remained of formality disappeared and the hours flowed easily down the profuse stream of champagne. In the modern fashion, Hamilton Rutherford sat at the table with his arm round an old girl of his and assured his guests, which included not a few bewildered but enthusiastic Europeans, that the party was not nearly at an end; it was to reassemble at Zelli's after midnight. Michael saw Mrs Dandy, not quite over her illness, rise to go and become caught in polite group after group, and he spoke of it to one of her daughters, who thereupon forcibly abducted her mother and called her car. Michael felt very considerate and proud of himself after having done this, and drank much more champagne.

'It's amazing,' George Packman was telling him enthusiastically. 'This show will cost Ham about five thousand dollars, and I understand they'll be just about his last. But did he countermand a bottle of champagne or a flower? Not he! He happens to have it – that young man. Do you know that T.G. Vance offered him a salary of fifty thousand dollars a year ten minutes before the wedding this morning? In another year he'll be back with the millionaires.'

The conversation was interrupted by a plan to carry Rutherford out on communal shoulders – a plan which six of them put into effect, and then stood in the four-o'clock sunshine waving goodbye to the bride and groom. But there must have been a mistake somewhere, for five minutes later Michael saw both bride and groom descending the stairway to the reception, each with a glass of champagne held defiantly on high.

'This is our way of doing things,' he thought. 'Generous and fresh and free; a sort of Virginia-plantation hospitality, but at a different pace now, nervous as ticker tape.'

Standing unselfconsciously in the middle of the room to see which was the American ambassador, he realised with a start that he hadn't really thought of Caroline for hours. He looked about him with a sort of alarm, and then he saw her across the room, very bright and young, and radiantly happy. He saw Rutherford near her, looking at her as if he could never look long enough, and as Michael watched them they seemed to recede as he had wished them to do that day in the rue de Castiglione – recede and fade off into joys and griefs of their own, into the years that would take the toll of Rutherford's fine pride and Caroline's young, moving beauty; fade far away, so that now he could scarcely see them, as if they were shrouded in something as misty as her white, billowing dress.

Michael was cured. The ceremonial function, with its pomp and its revelry, had stood for a sort of initiation into a life where even his regret could not follow them. All the bitterness melted out of him suddenly and the world reconstituted itself out of the youth and happiness that was all around him, profligate as the spring sunshine. He was trying to remember which of the bridesmaids he had made a date to dine with tonight as he walked forward to bid Hamilton and Caroline goodbye.

# The Last of the Belles

# 1

After Atlanta's elaborate and theatrical rendition of Southern charm, we all underestimated Tarleton. It was a little hotter than anywhere we'd been – a dozen rookies collapsed the first day in that Georgia sun – and when you saw herds of cows drifting through the business streets, hi-yaed by coloured drovers, a trance stole down over you out of the hot light: you wanted to move a hand or foot to be sure you were alive.

So I stayed out at camp and let Lieutenant Warren tell me about the girls. This was fifteen years ago, and I've forgotten how I felt, except that the days went along, one after another, better than they do now, and I was empty-hearted, because up North she whose legend I had loved for three years was getting married. I saw the clippings and newspaper photographs. It was 'a romantic wartime wedding', all very rich and sad. I felt vividly the dark radiance of the sky under which it took place and, as a young snob, was more envious than sorry.

A day came when I went into Tarleton for a haircut and ran into a nice fellow named Bill Knowles, who was in my time at Harvard. He'd been in the National Guard division that preceded us in camp; at the last moment he had transferred to aviation and had been left behind.

'I'm glad I met you, Andy,' he said with undue seriousness. 'I'll hand you on all my information before I start for Texas. You see, there're really only three girls here –'

I was interested; there was something mystical about there being three girls.

'– and here's one of them now.'

We were in front of a drug store and he marched me in and introduced me to a lady I promptly detested.

'The other two are Ailie Calhoun and Sally Carrol Happer.'

I guessed from the way he pronounced her name that he was interested in Ailie Calhoun. It was on his mind what she would be doing while he was gone; he wanted her to have a quiet, uninteresting time.

At my age I don't even hesitate to confess that entirely unchivalrous images of Ailie Calhoun – that lovely name – rushed into my mind. At twenty-three there is no such thing as a pre-empted beauty; though, had Bill asked me, I would doubtless have sworn in all my sincerity to care for her like a sister. He didn't; he was just fretting out loud at having to go. Three days later he telephoned me that he was leaving next morning and he'd take me to her house that night.

We met at the hotel and walked uptown through the flowery, hot twilight. The four white pillars of the Calhoun house faced the street, and behind them the veranda was dark as a cave with hanging, weaving, climbing vines.

When we came up the walk a girl in a white dress tumbled out of the front door, crying, 'I'm so sorry I'm late!' and seeing us, added: 'Why, I thought I heard you come ten minutes –'

She broke off as a chair creaked and another man, an aviator from Camp Harry Lee, emerged from the obscurity of the veranda.

'Why, Canby!' she cried. 'How are you?'

He and Bill Knowles waited with the tenseness of open litigants.

'Canby, I want to whisper to you, honey,' she said, after just a second. 'You'll excuse us, Bill.'

They went aside. Presently Lieutenant Canby, immensely displeased, said in a grim voice, 'Then we'll make it Thursday, but that means sure.' Scarcely nodding to us, he went down the walk, the spurs with which he presumably urged on his aeroplane gleaming in the lamplight.

'Come in – I don't just know your name –'

There she was – the Southern type in all its purity. I would have recognised Ailie Calhoun if I'd never heard Ruth Draper or read Marse Chan. She had the adroitness sugar-coated with sweet, voluble simplicity, the suggested background of devoted fathers, brothers and admirers stretching back into the South's heroic age, the unfailing coolness acquired in the endless struggle with the heat. There were notes in her voice that ordered slaves around, that withered up Yankee captains, and then soft, wheedling notes that mingled in unfamiliar loveliness with the night.

I could scarcely see her in the darkness, but when I rose to go – it was plain that I was not to linger – she stood in the orange light from the doorway. She was small and very blond; there was too much fever-coloured rouge on her face, accentuated by a nose dabbed clownish white, but she shone through that like a star.

'After Bill goes I'll be sitting here all alone night after night. Maybe you'll take me to the country-club dances.' The pathetic prophecy brought a laugh from Bill. 'Wait a minute,' Ailie murmured. 'Your guns are all crooked.'

She straightened my collar pin, looking up at me for a second with something more than curiosity. It was a seeking look, as if she asked, 'Could it be you?' Like Lieutenant Canby, I marched off unwillingly into the suddenly insufficient night.

Two weeks later I sat with her on the same veranda, or rather she half lay in my arms and yet scarcely touched me – how she managed that I don't remember. I was trying unsuccessfully to kiss her, and had been trying for the best part of an hour. We had a sort of joke about my not being sincere. My theory was that if she'd let me kiss her I'd fall in love with her. Her argument was that I was obviously insincere.

In a lull between two of these struggles she told me about her brother who had died in his senior year at Yale. She showed me his picture – it was a handsome, earnest face with a Leyendecker forelock – and told me that when she met someone who measured up to him she'd marry. I found this family idealism discouraging; even my brash confidence couldn't compete with the dead.

The evening and other evenings passed like that, and ended with my going back to camp with the remembered smell of magnolia flowers and a mood of vague dissatisfaction. I never kissed her. We went to the vaudeville and to the country club on Saturday nights, where she seldom took ten consecutive steps with one man, and she took me to barbecues and rowdy watermelon parties, and never thought it worthwhile to change what I felt for her into love. I see now that it wouldn't have been hard, but she was a wise nineteen and she must have seen that we were emotionally incompatible. So I became her confidant instead.

We talked about Bill Knowles. She was considering Bill; for, though she wouldn't admit it, a winter at school in New York and a prom at Yale had turned her eyes North. She said she didn't think she'd marry a Southern man. And by degrees I saw that she was consciously and voluntarily different from these other girls who sang nigger songs and shot craps in the country-club bar. That's why Bill and I and others were drawn to her. We recognised her.

June and July, while the rumours reached us faintly, ineffectually, of battle and terror overseas, Ailie's eyes roved here and there about the country-club floor, seeking for something among the tall young officers. She attached several, choosing them with unfailing perspicacity – save in the case of Lieutenant Canby, whom she claimed to despise, but, nevertheless, gave dates to 'because he was so sincere' – and we apportioned her evenings among us all summer.

One day she broke all her dates – Bill Knowles had leave and was coming. We talked of the event with scientific impersonality – would he move her to a decision? Lieutenant Canby, on the contrary, wasn't impersonal at all; made a nuisance of himself. He told her that if she married Knowles he was going to climb up six thousand feet in his aeroplane, shut off the motor and let go. He frightened her – I had to yield him my last date before Bill came.

On Saturday night she and Bill Knowles came to the country club. They were very handsome together and once more I felt envious and sad. As they danced out on the floor the three-piece orchestra was playing 'After You've Gone', in a poignant incomplete way that I can hear yet, as if each bar were trickling off a precious minute of that time. I knew then that I had grown to love Tarleton, and I glanced about half in panic to see if some face wouldn't come in for me out of that warm, singing, outer darkness that yielded up couple after couple in organdie and olive drab. It was a time of youth and war, and there was never so much love around.

When I danced with Ailie she suddenly suggested that we go outside to a car. She wanted to know why didn't people cut in on her tonight? Did they think she was already married?

'Are you going to be?'

'I don't know, Andy. Sometimes, when he treats me as if I were sacred, it thrills me.' Her voice was hushed and far away. 'And then –'

She laughed. Her body, so frail and tender, was touching mine, her face was turned up to me, and there, suddenly, with Bill Knowles ten yards off, I could have kissed her at last.

Our lips just touched experimentally; then an aviation officer turned a corner of the veranda near us, peered into our darkness and hesitated.

'Ailie.'

'Yes.'

'You heard about this afternoon?'

'What?' she leant forward, tenseness already in her voice.

'Horace Canby crashed. He was instantly killed.'

She got up slowly and stepped out of the car.

'You mean he was killed?' she said.

'Yes. They don't know what the trouble was. His motor –'

'Oh-h-h!' Her rasping whisper came through the hands suddenly covering her face. We watched her helplessly as she put her head on the side of the car, gagging dry tears. After a minute I went for Bill, who was standing in the stag line, searching anxiously about for her, and told him she wanted to go home.

I sat on the steps outside. I had disliked Canby, but his terrible, pointless death was more real to me then than the day's toll of thousands in France. In a few minutes Ailie and Bill came out. Ailie was whimpering a little, but when she saw me her eyes flexed and she came over swiftly.

'Andy' – she spoke in a quick, low voice – 'of course you must never tell anybody what I told you about Canby yesterday. What he said, I mean.'

'Of course not.'

She looked at me a second longer as if to be quite sure. Finally she was sure. Then she sighed in such a quaint little way that I could hardly believe my ears, and her brow went up in what can only be described as mock despair.

'An-dy!'

I looked uncomfortably at the ground, aware that she was

calling my attention to her involuntarily disastrous effect on men.

'Goodnight, Andy!' called Bill as they got into a taxi.

'Goodnight,' I said, and almost added: 'You poor fool.'


2


Of course I should have made one of those fine moral decisions that people make in books, and despised her. On the contrary, I don't doubt that she could still have had me by raising her hand.

A few days later she made it all right by saying wistfully, 'I know you think it was terrible of me to think of myself at a time like that, but it was such a shocking coincidence.'

At twenty-three I was entirely unconvinced about anything, except that some people were strong and attractive and could do what they wanted, and others were caught and disgraced. I hoped I was of the former. I was sure Ailie was.

I had to revise other ideas about her. In the course of a long discussion with some girl about kissing – in those days people still talked about kissing more than they kissed – I mentioned the fact that Ailie had only kissed two or three men, and only when she thought she was in love. To my considerable discon-certion the girl figuratively just lay on the floor and howled.

'But it's true,' I assured her, suddenly knowing it wasn't. 'She told me herself.'

'Ailie Calhoun! Oh, my heavens! Why, last year at the Tech spring house party? –'

This was in September. We were going overseas any week now, and to bring us up to full strength a last batch of officers from the fourth training camp arrived. The fourth camp wasn't like the first three – the candidates were from the ranks; even from the drafted divisions. They had queer names without vowels in them, and save for a few young militiamen, you couldn't take it for granted that they came out of any background at all. The addition to our company was Lieutenant Earl Schoen from New Bedford, Massachusetts: as fine a physical specimen as I have ever seen. He was six-foot-three, with black hair, high colour and glossy dark-brown eyes. He wasn't very smart and he was definitely illiterate, yet he was a good officer, high-tempered and commanding, and with that becoming touch of vanity that sits well on the military. I had an idea that New Bedford was a country town, and set down his bumptious qualities to that.

We were doubled up in living quarters and he came into my hut. Inside of a week there was a cabinet photograph of some Tarleton girl nailed brutally to the shack wall.

'She's no jane or anything like that. She's a society girl: goes with all the best people here.'

The following Sunday afternoon I met the lady at a semi-private swimming pool in the country. When Ailie and I arrived, there was Schoen's muscular body rippling out of a bathing-suit at the far end of the pool.

'Hey, lieutenant!'

When I waved back at him he grinned and winked, jerking his head towards the girl at his side. Then, digging her in the ribs, he jerked his head at me. It was a form of introduction.

'Who's that with Kitty Preston?' Ailie asked, and when I told her she said he looked like a streetcar conductor, and pretended to look for her transfer.

A moment later he crawled powerfully and gracefully down the pool and pulled himself up at our side. I introduced him to Ailie.

'How do you like my girl, lieutenant?' he demanded. 'I told you she was all right, didn't I?' He jerked his head towards Ailie, this time to indicate that his girl and Ailie moved in the same circles. 'How about us all having dinner together down at the hotel some night?'

I left them in a moment, amused as I saw Ailie visibly making up her mind that here, anyhow, was not the ideal. But Lieutenant Earl Schoen was not to be dismissed so lightly. He ran his eyes cheerfully and inoffensively over her cute, slight figure, and decided that she would do even better than the other. Then minutes later I saw them in the water together, Ailie swimming away with a grim little stroke she had, and Schoen wallowing riotously around her and ahead of her, sometimes pausing and staring at her, fascinated, as a boy might look at a nautical doll.

While the afternoon passed he remained at her side. Finally Ailie came over to me and whispered, with a laugh: 'He's a-following me around. He thinks I haven't paid my car fare.'

She turned quickly. Miss Kitty Preston, her face curiously flustered, stood facing us.

'Ailie Calhoun, I didn't think it of you to go out and delib'ately try to take a man away from another girl.' – An expression of distress at the impending scene flitted over Ailie's face – 'I thought you considered yourself above anything like that.'

Miss Preston's voice was low, but it held that tensity that can be felt further than it can be heard, and I saw Ailie's clear lovely eyes glance about in panic. Luckily, Earl himself was ambling cheerfully and innocently towards us.

'If you care for him you certainly oughtn't to belittle yourself in front of him,' said Ailie in a flash, her head high.

It was her acquaintance with the traditional way of behaving against Kitty Preston's naive and fierce possessiveness, or if you prefer it, Ailie's 'breeding' against the other's 'commonness'. She turned away.

'Wait a minute, kid!' cried Earl Schoen. 'How about your address? Maybe I'd like to give you a ring on the phone.'

She looked at him in a way that should have indicated to Kitty her entire lack of interest.

'I'm very busy at the Red Cross this month,' she said, her voice as cool as her slicked-back blond hair. 'Goodbye.'

On the way home she laughed. Her air of having been unwittingly involved in a contemptible business vanished.

'She'll never hold that young man,' she said. 'He wants somebody new.'

'Apparently he wants Ailie Calhoun.'

The idea amused her.

'He could give me his ticket punch to wear, like a fraternity pin. What fun! If Mother ever saw anybody like that come in the house, she'd just lie down and die.'

And to give Ailie credit, it was fully a fortnight before he did come to her house, although she rushed her until she pretended to be annoyed at the next country-club dance.

'He's the biggest tough, Andy,' she whispered to me. 'But he's so sincere.'

She used the word 'tough' without the conviction it would have carried had he been a Southern boy. She only knew it with her mind; her ear couldn't distinguish between one Yankee voice and another. And somehow Mrs Calhoun didn't expire at his appearance on the threshold. The supposedly ineradicable prejudices of Ailie's parents were a convenient phenomenon that disappeared at her wish. It was her friends who were astonished. Ailie, always a little above Tarleton, whose beaus had been very carefully the 'nicest' men of the camp – Ailie and Lieutenant Schoen! I grew tired of assuring people that she was merely distracting herself – and indeed every week or so there was someone new – an ensign from Pensacola, an old friend from New Orleans – but always, in between times, there was Earl Schoen.

Orders arrived for an advance party of officers and sergeants to proceed to the port of embarkation and take ship to France. My name was on the list. I had been on the range for a week and when I got back to camp, Earl Schoen buttonholed me immediately.

'We're giving a little farewell party in the mess. Just you and I and Captain Craker and three girls.'

Earl and I were to call for the girls. We picked up Sally Carrol Happer and Nancy Lamar, and went on to Ailie's house; to be met at the door by the butler with the announcement that she wasn't home.

'Isn't home?' Earl repeated blankly. 'Where is she?'

'Didn't leave no information about that; just said she wasn't home.'

'But this is a darn funny thing!' he exclaimed. He walked around the familiar dusky veranda while the butler waited at the door. Something occurred to him. 'Say,' he informed me – 'say, I think she's sore.'

I waited. He said sternly to the butler, 'You tell her I've got to speak to her a minute.'

'How'm I goin' tell her that when she ain't home?'

Again Earl walked musingly around the porch. Then he nodded several times and said:

'She's sore at something that happened downtown.'

In a few words he sketched out the matter to me.

'Look here; you wait in the car,' I said. 'Maybe I can fix this.'

And when he reluctantly retreated: 'Oliver, you tell Miss Ailie I want to see her alone.'

After some argument he bore this message and in a moment returned with a reply:

'Miss Ailie say she don't want to see that other gentleman about nothing never. She say come in if you like.'

She was in the library. I had expected to see a picture of cool, outraged dignity, but her face was distraught, tumultuous, despairing. Her eyes were red-rimmed, as though she had been crying slowly and painfully, for hours.

'Oh, hello, Andy,' she said brokenly. 'I haven't seen you for so long. Has he gone?'

'Now, Ailie –'

'Now, Ailie!' she cried. 'Now, Ailie! He spoke to me, you see. He lifted his hat. He stood there ten feet from me with that horrible – that horrible woman – holding her arm and talking to her, and then when he saw me he raised his hat. Andy, I didn't know what to do. I had to go in the drug store and ask for a glass of water, and I was so afraid he'd follow in after me that I asked Mr Rich to let me go out the back way. I never want to see him or hear of him again.'

I talked. I said what one says in such cases. I said it for half an hour. I could not move her. Several times she answered by murmuring something about his not being 'sincere', and for the fourth time I wondered what the word meant to her. Certainly not constancy; it was, I half suspected, some special way she wanted to be regarded.

I got up to go. And then, unbelievably, the automobile horn sounded three times impatiently outside. It was stupefying. It said as plainly as if Earl were in the room, 'All right; go to the devil then! I'm not going to wait here all night.'

Ailie looked at me aghast. And suddenly a peculiar

look came into her face, spread, flickered, broke into a teary, hysterical smile.

'Isn't he awful?' she cried in helpless despair. 'Isn't he terrible?'

'Hurry up,' I said quickly. 'Get your cape. This is our last night.'

And I can still feel that last night vividly, the candlelight that flickered over the rough boards of the mess shack, over the frayed paper decorations left from the supply company's party, the sad mandolin down a company street that kept picking 'My Indiana Home' out of the universal nostalgia of the departing summer. The three girls lost in this mysterious men's city felt something, too – a bewitched impermanence as though they were on a magic carpet that had lighted on the Southern countryside, and any moment the wind would lift it and waft it away. We toasted ourselves and the South. Then we left our napkins and empty glasses and a little of the past on the table, and hand in hand went out into the moonlight itself. Taps had been played; there was no sound but the far-away whinny of a horse, and a loud persistent snore at which we laughed, and the leathery snap of a sentry coming to port over by the guardhouse. Craker was on duty; we others got into a waiting car, motored into Tarleton and left Craker's girl.

Then Ailie and Earl, Sally and I, two and two in the wide back seat, each couple turned from the other, absorbed and whispering, drove away into the wide, flat darkness.

We drove through pine woods heavy with lichen and Spanish moss, and between the fallow cotton fields along a road white as the rim of the world. We parked under the broken shadow of a mill where there was the sound of running water and restive squawky birds and over everything a brightness that tried to filter in anywhere – into the lost nigger cabins, the automobile, the fastnesses of the heart. The South sang to us – I wonder if they remember. I remember – the cool pale faces, the somnolent amorous eyes and the voices:

'Are you comfortable?'

'Yes; are you?'

'Are you sure you are?'

'Yes.'

Suddenly we knew it was late and there was nothing more. We turned home.

Our detachment started for Camp Mills next day, but I didn't go to France after all. We passed a cold month on Long Island, marched aboard a transport with steel helmets slung at our sides and then marched off again. There wasn't any more war. I had missed the war. When I came back to Tarleton I tried to get out of the army, but I had a regular commission and it took most of the winter. But Earl Schoen was one of the first to be demobilised. He wanted to find a good job 'while the picking was good'. Ailie was non-committal, but there was an understanding between them that he'd be back.

By January the camps, which for two years had dominated the little city, were already fading. There was only the persistent incinerator smell to remind one of all that activity and bustle. What life remained centred bitterly about divisional headquarters building with the disgruntled regular officers who had also missed the war.

And now the young men of Tarleton began drifting back from the ends of the earth – some with Canadian uniforms, some with crutches or empty sleeves. A returned battalion of the National Guard paraded through the streets with open ranks for their dead, and then stepped down out of romance for ever and sold you things over the counters of local stores.

Only a few uniforms mingled with the dinner coats at the country-club dance.

Just before Christmas, Bill Knowles arrived unexpectedly one day and left the next – either he gave Ailie an ultimatum or she had made up her mind at last. I saw her sometimes when she wasn't busy with returned heroes from Savannah and Augusta, but I felt like an outmoded survival – and I was. She was waiting for Earl Schoen with such a vast uncertainty that she didn't like to talk about it. Three days before I got my final discharge he came.

I first happened upon them walking down Market Street together, and I don't think I've ever been so sorry for a couple in my life; though I suppose the same situation was repeating itself in every city where there had been camps. Exteriorly Earl had about everything wrong with him that could be imagined. His hat was green, with a radical feather; his suit was slashed and braided in a grotesque fashion that national advertising and the movies have put an end to. Evidently he had been to his old barber, for his hair bloused neatly on his pink, shaved neck. It wasn't as though he had been shiny and poor, but the background of mill-town dance halls and outing clubs flamed out at you – or rather flamed out at Ailie. For she had never quite imagined the reality; in these clothes even the natural grace of that magnificent body had departed. At first he boasted of his fine job; it would get them along all right until he could 'see some easy money'. But from the moment he came back into her world on its own terms he must have known it was hopeless. I don't know what Ailie said or how much her grief weighed against her stupefaction. She acted quickly – three days after his arrival, Earl and I went North together on the train.

'Well, that's the end of that,' he said moodily. 'She's a

wonderful girl, but too much of a highbrow for me. I guess she's got to marry some rich guy that'll give her a great social position. I can't see that stuck-up sort of thing.' And then, later: 'She said to come back and see her in a year, but I'll never go back. This aristocrat stuff is all right if you got the money for it, but –'

'But it wasn't real,' he meant to finish. The provincial society in which he had moved with so much satisfaction for six months already appeared to him as affected, 'dudish' and artificial.

'Say, did you see what I saw getting on the train?' he asked me after a while. 'Two wonderful janes, all alone. What do you say we mosey into the next car and ask them to lunch? I'll take the one in blue.' Halfway down the car he turned around suddenly. 'Say, Andy,' he demanded, frowning; 'one thing – how do you suppose she knew I used to command a streetcar? I never told her that.'

'Search me.'

3

This narrative arrives now at one of the big gaps that stared me in the face when I began. For six years, while I finished at Harvard Law and built commercial aeroplanes and backed a pavement block that went gritty under trucks, Ailie Calhoun was scarcely more than a name on a Christmas card; something that blew a little in my mind on warm nights when I remembered the magnolia flowers. Occasionally an acquaintance of army days would ask me, 'What became of that blond girl who was so popular?' but I didn't know. I ran into Nancy Lamar at the Montmartre in New York one evening and learnt that Ailie had become engaged to a man in Cincinnati, had gone North to visit his family and then broken it off. She was lovely as ever and there was always a heavy beau or two. But neither Bill Knowles nor Earl Schoen had ever come back.

And somewhere about that time I heard that Bill Knowles had married a girl he met on a boat. There you are – not much of a patch to mend six years with.

Oddly enough, a girl seen at twilight in a small Indiana station started me thinking about going South. The girl, in stiff pink organdie, threw her arms about a man who got off our train and hurried him to a waiting car, and I felt a sort of pang. It seemed to me that she was bearing him off into the lost midsummer world of my early twenties, where time had stood still and charming girls, dimly seen like the past itself, still loitered along the dusky streets. I suppose that poetry is a Northern man's dream of the South. But it was months later that I sent off a wire to Ailie, and immediately followed it to Tarleton.

It was July. The Jefferson Hotel seemed strangely shabby and stuffy – a boosters' club burst into intermittent song in the dining-room that my memory had long dedicated to officers and girls. I recognised the taxi driver who took me up to Ailie's house, but his 'Sure, I do, lieutenant' was unconvincing. I was only one of twenty thousand.

It was a curious three days. I suppose some of Ailie's first young lustre must have gone the way of such mortal shining, but I can't bear witness to it. She was still so physically appealing that you wanted to touch the personality that trembled on her lips. No – the change was more profound than that.

At once I saw she had a different line. The modulations of

pride, the vocal hints that she knew the secrets of a brighter, finer ante-bellum day, were gone from her voice; there was no time for them now as it rambled on in the half-laughing, half-desperate banter of the newer South. And everything was swept into this banter in order to make it go on and leave no time for thinking – the present, the future, herself, me. We went to a rowdy party at the house of some young married people, and she was the nervous, glowing centre of it. After all, she wasn't eighteen, and she was as attractive in her role of reckless clown as she had ever been in her life.

'Have you heard anything from Earl Schoen?' I asked her the second night, on our way to the country-club dance.

'No.' She was serious for a moment. 'I often think of him. He was the –' She hesitated.

'Go on.'

'I was going to say the man I loved most, but that wouldn't be true. I never exactly loved him, or I'd have married him any old how, wouldn't I?' She looked at me questioningly. 'At least I wouldn't have treated him like that.'

'It was impossible.'

'Of course,' she agreed uncertainly. Her mood changed; she became flippant: 'How the Yankees did deceive us poor little Southern girls. Ah, me!'

When we reached the country club she melted like a chameleon into the – to me – unfamiliar crowd. There was a new generation upon the floor, with less dignity than the ones I had known, but none of them was more a part of its lazy, feverish essence than Ailie. Possibly she had perceived that in her initial longing to escape from Tarleton's provincialism she had been walking alone, following a generation which was doomed to have no successors. Just where she lost the battle, waged behind the white pillars of her veranda, I don't know.

But she had guessed wrong, missed out somewhere. Her wild animation, which even now called enough men around her to rival the entourage of the youngest and freshest, was an admission of defeat.

I left her house, as I had so often left it that vanished June, in a mood of vague dissatisfaction. It was hours later, tossing about my bed in the hotel, that I realised what was the matter, what had always been the matter – I was deeply and incurably in love with her. In spite of every incompatibility, she was still, she would always be to me, the most attractive girl I had ever known. I told her so next afternoon. It was one of those hot days I knew so well, and Ailie sat beside me on a couch in the darkened library.

'Oh, no, I couldn't marry you,' she said, almost frightened; 'I don't love you that way at all... I never did. And you don't love me. I didn't mean to tell you now, but next month I'm going to marry another man. We're not even announcing it, because I've done that twice before.' Suddenly it occurred to her that I might be hurt: 'Andy, you just had a silly idea, didn't you? You know I couldn't ever marry a Northern man.'

'Who is he?' I demanded.

'A man from Savannah.'

'Are you in love with him?'

'Of course I am.' We both smiled. 'Of course I am! What are you trying to make me say?'

There were no doubts, as there had been with other men. She couldn't afford to let herself have doubts. I knew this because she had long ago stopped making any pretensions with me. This very naturalness, I realised, was because she didn't consider me as a suitor. Beneath her mask of an instinctive thoroughbred she had always been on to herself, and she couldn't believe that anyone not taken in to the point of uncritical worship could really love her. That was what she called being 'sincere'; she felt most security with men like Canby and Earl Schoen, who were incapable of passing judgements on the ostensibly aristocratic heart.

'All right,' I said, as if she had asked my permission to marry. 'Now, would you do something for me?'

'Anything.'

'Ride out to camp.'

'But there's nothing left there, honey.'

'I don't care.'

We walked downtown. The taxi driver in front of the hotel repeated her objection: 'Nothing there now, cap.'

'Never mind. Go there anyhow.'

Twenty minutes later he stopped on a wide unfamiliar plain powdered with new cotton fields and marked with isolated clumps of pine.

'Like to drive over yonder where you see the smoke?' asked the driver. 'That's the new state prison.'

'No. Just drive along this road. I want to find where I used to live.'

An old racecourse, inconspicuous in the camp's day of glory, had reared its dilapidated grandstand in the desolation. I tried in vain to orient myself.

'Go along this road past that clump of trees, and then turn right – no, turn left.'

He obeyed, with professional disgust.

'You won't find a single thing, darling,' said Ailie. 'The contractors took it all down.'

We rode slowly along the margin of the fields. It might have been here –

'All right. I want to get out,' I said suddenly.

I left Ailie sitting in the car, looking very beautiful with the warm breeze stirring her long, curly bob.

It might have been here. That would make the company streets down there and the mess shack, where we dined that night, just over the way.

The taxi driver regarded me indulgently while I stumbled here and there in the knee-deep underbrush, looking for my youth in a clapboard or a strip of roofing or a rusty tomato can. I tried to sight on a vaguely familiar clump of trees, but it was growing darker now and I couldn't be quite sure they were the right trees.

'They're going to fix up the old racecourse,' Ailie called from the car. 'Tarleton's getting quite doggy in its old age.'

No. Upon consideration they didn't look like the right trees. All I could be sure of was this place that had once been so full of life and effort was gone, as if it had never existed, and that in another month Ailie would be gone, and the South would be empty for me for ever.

Francis Scott Key Fitzgerald was born in 1896 in St Paul, Minnesota. His parents were middle class, but not particularly wealthy and had to save to put Fitzgerald through private school and Princeton University. Ambitious to become a writer, Fitzgerald neglected his studies, was put on academic probation, and in 1917 left Princeton to join the army. Shortly before his posting, he submitted his first manuscript, 'The Romantic Egotist', to Scribners; it was rejected, but with a letter encouraging him to rework and resubmit the story.

In 1918, Fitzgerald was posted to Camp Sheridan in Alabama. He was never sent abroad to active service, but during his time in the South, he met and fell in love with Zelda Sayre, the eighteen-year-old daughter of a local judge. They became engaged, and Scribners' final acceptance of Fitzgerald's manuscript – now titled *This Side of Paradise* – in 1919, financed their marriage the following year. The novel dealt with the boredom and disillusionment of the social elite at Princeton after the war, and brought Fitzgerald immediate acclaim. The Fitzgeralds embarked on a life of social excess in New York, and though a number of short stories and a second novel, *The Beautiful and the Damned* (1922), followed in the next two years, Fitzgerald's critical image was compromised by their extravagant lifestyle.

The Fitzgeralds moved back to Minnesota for the birth of their daughter Frances Scott Fitzgerald in 1921. They returned to New York in 1922, but the social life remained a distraction and hampered Fitzgerald's attempts at writing. Finally in 1924, the family moved to France, seeking a more subdued atmosphere, and here, in Valescure on the Côte d'Azur, Fitzgerald wrote *The Great Gatsby*. This novel, widely considered his masterpiece, deals with his perennial themes of money, class, and jazz-age social degeneration, and has been hailed as a candidate for the 'great American novel'.

The Fitzgeralds remained in France for the next three years, alternating between the Riviera and Paris, where Fitzgerald met the then little-known Ernest Hemingway, but the atmosphere of France proved unconducive both to the Fitzgerald's writing and to Zelda's mental health. After a brief return to America, Zelda suffered her first breakdown in 1930 and was moved to a Swiss clinic for treatment, which Fitzgerald financed with the proceeds from new short stories.

The Fitzgeralds moved back to America permanently in 1931, and the fourth novel was finally finished three years later. *Tender is the Night* is the story of a psychologist and his damaging marriage to a schizophrenic, and it reflected his unease with his own marriage to Zelda, who was now frequently in and out of mental institutions and had published her own autobiographical novel, *Save Me the Waltz*, in 1932. The new novel was not a commercial success and, by the mid-1930s, Fitzgerald was in serious financial difficulty. After a period spent in hotels in North Carolina, where Zelda was in Highland Hospital, he moved to Hollywood to work on film adaptations and screenplays. His final novel, *The Love of the Last Tycoon*, was inspired by his experiences in Hollywood, but was left unfinished when he died of a heart attack in 1940.

# HESPERUS PRESS – 100 PAGES

Hesperus Press, as suggested by the Latin motto, is committed to bringing near what is far – far both in space and time. Works written by the greatest authors, and unjustly neglected or simply little known in the English-speaking world, are made accessible through new translations and a completely fresh editorial approach. Through these short classic works, each around 100 pages in length, the reader will be introduced to the greatest writers from all times and all cultures.

For more information on Hesperus Press, please visit our website: **www.hesperuspress.com**

ET REMOTISSIMA PROPE

## SELECTED TITLES FROM HESPERUS PRESS

Gustave Flaubert *Memoirs of a Madman*

Alexander Pope *Scriblerus*

Ugo Foscolo *Last Letters of Jacopo Ortis*

Anton Chekhov *The Story of a Nobody*

Joseph von Eichendorff *Life of a Good-for-nothing*

Mark Twain *The Diary of Adam and Eve*

Giovanni Boccaccio *Life of Dante*

Victor Hugo *The Last Day of a Condemned Man*

Joseph Conrad *Heart of Darkness*

Edgar Allan Poe *Eureka*

Emile Zola *For a Night of Love*

Daniel Defoe *The King of Pirates*

Giacomo Leopardi *Thoughts*

Nikolai Gogol *The Squabble*

Franz Kafka *Metamorphosis*

Herman Melville *The Enchanted Isles*

Leonardo da Vinci *Prophecies*

Charles Baudelaire *On Wine and Hashish*

William Makepeace Thackeray *Rebecca and Rowena*

Wilkie Collins *Who Killed Zebedee?*

Théophile Gautier *The Jinx*

Charles Dickens *The Haunted House*

Luigi Pirandello *Loveless Love*

Fyodor Dostoevsky *Poor People*

E.T.A. Hoffmann *Mademoiselle de Scudéri*

Henry James *In the Cage*

Francis Petrarch *My Secret Book*

André Gide *Theseus*

D.H. Lawrence *The Fox*

Percy Bysshe Shelley *Zastrozzi*